NASHVILLE DAYS

JULIE CAPULET

**Every song he wrote was about a girl he hadn't
met yet. Then she walked into his life.**

Travis Tucker is a country-rock superstar. With four
number one albums, sold-out tours and millions of fans,
he's living the dream. But somewhere along the way, the
spotlight lost its shine. Travis can never find the one thing
he's been writing all his songs about: *real* love. So he
decides to buy himself a country getaway to work on his
next record and clear his head.

Ruby Hayes is a small town girl with big dreams. Finally
free of boarding school, she plans on spending the
summer writing songs on the piano in the abandoned
farmhouse next door. Then she's on her way to Nashville.

When Travis finds Ruby, singing like an angel at his
piano, he falls *hard*. Now that he's finally found the girl
he's been searching for, Ruby ignites in him a wild
obsession that's hotter than the Tennessee sun. And she
has no idea who he is.

For Ruby, things get complicated. With a voice that's
somehow familiar, like he's already a part of her, Travis is
a temptation she can't resist.

The summer becomes a feverish haze of hot nights,

shared lyrics, and the kind of spark that blazes into wildfire.

But summer can't last forever. Can their love survive beyond it, with the demands of Travis's high-profile life, Ruby's ambition and a jealous best friend threatening to come between them?

Or is this a love story written in both the music and the stars?

Nashville Days is a steamy standalone small town rockstar romance starring a hot, hopelessly romantic lead singer and the sweet & sassy songbird who steals his heart. Perfect for fans of Elsie Silver.

Music City Lovers

Nashville DAYS

1

TRAVIS

"I want to thank ya'll for coming out tonight, Austin. You know we love you." The crowd roars.

We play our last song, our newest number one hit. I can barely hear my own voice as a hundred thousand people sing along with me. It's a crazy feeling, having *this* many souls touched by your words and so fully invested, singing their goddamn hearts out. They know every note. They've lived their lives to these lyrics. They've loved, cried and laughed to these tunes. They're filling up the night with their emotion, swaying to the slow rhythm. The lights of their phones shine like a galaxy of stars.

And when we hit that final chord, the thundering cheer of the crowd is deafening. Vaughn climbs down from his drums and the three of us stand there together on stage for a few seconds, taking it all in. The applause of a hundred thousand people is something you don't ever really get used to. The adrenaline rush is just as pure as it was the very first time.

We take a final bow and exit the stage, where a swarm of security surrounds us and ushers us through a bullet-proof corridor toward our tour bus. I can still hear them chanting my name. But we've done our encores after playing for three and a half hours. We're getting close to the end of our 48-show, 38-city tour and I'm feeling it. The highs and lows and the creeping exhaustion that sets in after giving it everything you've got for months on end. We have two final shows left, both at home in Nashville. It's been by far our biggest tour yet.

I feel lit by the crowd, the music, the whiskey and the wine, the satisfaction of pouring my heart and soul into something real. Something that touches people and connects them. Every single show has been sold out. Our record is number one. Four of our songs are in the top ten. And the momentum just keeps on building.

We get to the bus and it's crowded, with groupies and people from the band and hangers-on. Our opening act, Jackson Cole, and his entourage are here, like they always seem to be. The fame and the women are new to him. He's overdosing and finding his feet, maybe. Riding our wave, to a certain extent, but whatever.

Vaughn pours three shots. Roxie gives Kade a hug, then me. She's relieved. Turns out our little sister is a genius at managing us. This tour has been bigger than we ever imagined. Now we can play our last two home shows and finally take a much-needed break before we start another 12-show West Coast tour next month.

I collapse onto one of the plush chairs. I tip back the whiskey Vaughn hands me. One of the groupies puts her hand on my arm and leans close to me. "Travis, you were amazing tonight. You're *so* good."

Do I know her? I don't think so. She might be a new one. It all starts to blur at the edges after a while. They all start looking the same. I'm no saint but I also need to *feel* something before I'll act on the constant stream of attention and adoration I happen to get. Right now I'm not feeling much of anything.

Kade hands me a beer.

"Hell," he says, sitting in the chair next to mine and clinking his bottle against mine. "Texas always has insane crowds. I could hardly even hear us." As usual, Kade's new-ish girlfriend Carmen is hovering around him. Roxie's not a fan. Come to think of it, neither am I. I don't usually care much who my brothers hang out with, but this girl seems to have an effect on Kade that's messing with his head. He's more moody when she's around. Jackson joked that she's our Yoko, waiting in the wings, whispering in his ear all the time about running away together so he can work on his solo album. I don't think that's his plan. Not now, anyway. We're on too much of a roll. And I can't worry about it tonight.

Vaughn laughs and cranks up the music, chugging from the bottle of Jack he's holding. He's got a fat joint in his other hand. A groupie with a lot of piercings and a ridiculously short skirt puts a pink pill on his tongue. Another girl is unbuttoning his shirt. His black hair is unkempt and long. His eyes are bloodshot, which makes them look even more blue than usual.

Roxie pulls one of the girls away from him. "What did you give him?" She pries Vaughn's mouth open but he grins at her, sort of guiltily.

"Too late," he says.

"*Vaughn*," Roxie scolds him. "Booze and weed is one thing. You said no drugs."

"Come on, Rox, I'm celebrating. Give me one night."

"*One* night? You've had three whole *months* of nights."

"I'll go cold turkey after the tour," Vaughn tells her. "I'll take a break."

We've all heard that one before. My brother is out of control, is what it boils down to. And he's only getting worse.

Vaughn has always walked a fine line. Like our father did, until it killed him. Kade and I can easily keep up with our younger brother when it comes to the whiskey— and usually do—most of the time. The difference is, we have downtimes. We lay off when we're not touring. We clean up when we feel like it.

Cleaning up isn't something Vaughn's done in a while. I'm not sure he's even capable of it at this point. Kade and Roxie and I have talked about it. We decided to finish the tour, then we'll sit him down and talk it through with him. Get him some help or check him in somewhere if need be.

None of which is happening tonight.

We're driving all night tonight so we can get back to Nashville in the morning. There's no doubt this party will still be going when we get there.

This bus has been the hub of our non-stop bender all the way through. We all got into a groove of it for the first month or two, but after a while you find yourself getting more and more strung out from the total lack of sleep and peace and quiet. Even before we left, we were hounded like this. We have a loft warehouse we've converted into apartments, a recording studio and an office headquarters in downtown Nashville. We tried to keep the location under wraps but our fans found out about it, like they always do.

"That show was mayhem," says Vaughn. Not that he minds. Mayhem might as well be Vaughn's middle name. As if to confirm this, he blows a couple of smoke rings at me.

Tonight I'm not in the mood to fight my way through crowds of people just so I can go to bed.

What I need is some real sleep. Uninterrupted by banging and knocking and people trying to get in.

I need a quiet place to hang out for a while, I decide. A secret getaway. An old house out in the country some-where, far from the city and the rabid fans and the never-ending parade of groupies, where there's space and fresh air and days with nothing to do except write. I can't remember the last time I was *alone* for more than a few hours at a time.

I'll find myself someplace off the beaten track, where no one even knows I'm there. I'll sleep and daydream and clear my head. Maybe Vaughn can spend some time there too, and dry out. And Kade, without the girlfriend. All three of us. We'll work on our next record. We'll write our masterpiece, uninterrupted.

I send a message to a real estate agent I sometimes use when I buy new properties. I have three houses: an apartment in Nashville that's part of our headquarters, my own house in Franklin outside Nashville that I need to get a lot more security for because people have set up fucking camps around the peripheral fences, and a condo in L.A. None of them will be either empty or quiet. I have a lot of friends and an open-door policy for the most part, which I'm now starting to severely regret. All my houses have become magnets for hangers-on and their non-stop parties.

I'm looking for another house, I text him. *A farm, maybe, at least a half hour outside Nashville. Something remote. Very private. Surrounded by a lot of land. Maybe with a barn or something I can soundproof and convert into a studio. ASAP.*

Three girls surround me. One of them touches the top button of my shirt. I'm not in the mood to party tonight, go figure. I'm strung out. *Burned* out. I'm twenty-five years old and I already feel like I'm hanging on to the end of a fraying rope. I've been burning the candle at both ends for as long as I can remember and I suddenly feel a new urge for some goddamn solitude.

One of the girls touches my hair. Another whispers in my ear. "You're *so* hot, Travis. I love you so much."

I don't even know her name.

One of the girls weaves her fingers through mine. "We want to show you something in one of the bedrooms, Travis. *All* of us."

My phone pings with a message. It's from my real estate agent. Damn, he's fast. "Maybe later." I don't know, maybe I've become jaded. I don't want to fuck just for the hell of it, not that I ever really did. I'm not an out of control player like Vaughn and I'm not a soulful romantic like Kade. I fall somewhere in the middle. I have a good time without getting serious.

But sometimes—like right now—it occurs to me that I never quite *feel* as much as I wish I did. Never in a way that makes you want to hang on to it or get excited about it or make it last. Never in a way you'd write a goddamn song about. Which is too bad. Because I write a lot of songs. Songs about falling in love and chasing after that one and only true love because you think your heart will break if you can't spend every hour of every day with her until you die.

The truth is, I'm just guessing. Because I've never experienced anything close to that kind of intensity. Which, tonight, feels sort of … sad. All these desperate souls, looking for that one magical, elusive person they can fall in love with to the point that nothing and no one else matters.

Most of them will never find it. *I* might never find it.

Which is sort of tragic when you think about it.

Like now. Women are literally hanging off me. And I feel exactly … nothing. No spark. No interest. Just … boredom. A craving for something *real*.

I stand up and move away, as much as I can in the smoky, noisy, jam-packed space. People are getting loose.

I check the message. *I've got a new listing you might want to see. It's been sitting empty for 4 years and needs some work but it's a premium property. Beaut house. 5 bedrooms. 40 mins east of Nville, remote. Sits on 100 fenced acres with its own pond, a large barn and 3 cabins. Listed at 3.5m. It's bank-owned and available immediately.*

I follow the link and scroll through the photos.

Wow. The place is mint, but he wasn't wrong. It looks dusty and unkempt. In a good way. In a no-one-will-ever-suspect-I'm-there kind of way. I'll leave it like that. I'll become a hermit for the next few weeks and completely tune out. There are pictures of the barn too. It's huge and rustic. And the old cabins, dotted around the property.

The offer is almost too fucking good to be true.

I text him back. *Let me know where to transfer the $. I'll pay cash tonight.*

I'll move in immediately. Hell, I'll drive out there as soon as we get back.

We exchange a few more messages. He confirms that the sale has gone through. He'll have the power turned on. He'll courier the keys so they're there by the time I get to Nashville.

A strange longing settles into me that feels almost like hope. More than that. An eerie sense that something's about to happen.

2

———

I STEP OFF THE BUS, waving for the last time as it pulls away onto our country road, leaving a trail of dust behind it. I run up the gravel driveway to my house. The screen door slams behind me. Momma's washing dishes at the sink and Gigi's at the table with one of her textbooks open, writing on a notepad.

They both look up. "Hi, honey," says Momma.

"Hi, Momma. Hi, Gi," I say, but I don't stop to talk. I saw them yesterday at my graduation ceremony and I've got a life to start living.

Right now.

This morning we had a final service and a farewell party, and that was the end of that. Four years of imprisonment at one of the strictest Catholic schools in Tennessee. The place is like a relic from a different time. No cell phones, no internet, no socializing. No exposure to all the things that could lead us astray, like boys, pop culture or—worst of all—music. It was that last detail most of all that's been the hardest to bear. I'd begged and pleaded to be allowed to go to a normal school. *Unless you've got a million dollars or a proposal, you'll stay put until you're eighteen,* my mother told me. Just like she'd told my three older sisters.

St. Mary's used to be a convent and it may as well still be one. The locks on the doors are as fortified as a medieval castle, sealing out bad influences, along with fun, reality and life in general.

Sending me and my three sisters there was Momma's last hope of keeping us from running wild after our Daddy died of a heart attack six years ago. His sawed-off shotgun still sits in the closet.

As it turns out, Momma's plan completely backfired with my two oldest sisters. Scarlett got knocked up by a hot mechanic from Knoxville around six months after she graduated. Her new husband has big, oily muscles and the bluest eyes you've ever seen. Their baby girl Clementine is adorable and Scarlett seems happy enough but who can tell with all that crying going on.

Rose is already heading in the same direction. She thought she *might* be pregnant a few weeks ago—turns out she's not, luckily, especially since her boyfriend is so busy he doesn't seem to have a lot of time for her, but I don't dare bring that up. She's head over heels in love with him. He promised he's going to ask her to marry him but he hasn't had a chance to get her a ring yet, she said.

I guess it just shows that all you need to do to bring out the promiscuous tendencies in a girl is to lock her up and tell her to resist every temptation known to womankind. As soon as she breaks free, there's only one thing she's going to want to do.

The day after Rose cried to Gi about *maybe* being pregnant, Gigi decided we needed to take matters into our own hands. We didn't tell Momma about it but Gi—uncharacteristically, since she's not usually a rule-breaker—forged a note and took me out of school for a few hours so we could go to the free clinic and get ourselves on the pill. *If Scarlett and Rose are anything to go by,* she said, *all they have to do is breathe in our direction and we'll be knocked up before we can say shotgun marriage.*

I didn't bother arguing with her or reminding her that I was still in prison at that point. I guess she figured since boys were calling our house and knocking on the door to talk to her, and because I only had a few weeks left before I graduated, that it was better to be safe than sorry.

Gigi, unlike my other sisters, doesn't go out with any of the boys who pursue her. She's waiting, she says. She wants to make something of herself before she gets attached. She's the calmest of my sisters, by a long shot. She's diligent and kind and she studies hard at the associate degree she's been working on. She's almost finished and soon she'll start the practical part of her training. Her goal is to become a social worker.

Helping people is Gi's thing. My closest sister has a selfless and compassionate way about her that's rare, I think. She's without a doubt the nicest person I know. But, like all of us, there's a hint of a taste for the devil under all that sweetness. I see it every now and then. Sometimes when the sun is hot or the moon is bright, I get a glimpse of a wilder side to Gi that's waiting to be discovered. My bet is that once she finds the right guy, she'll wow him so much he'll give her anything she wants. She's unique, she's beautiful and whoever ends up winning her heart will be the luckiest man in the world. She hasn't found him yet, though, but I guess she wants to be ready just in case he shows up when she's least expecting it.

It's true that we're sort of famous. Or infamous. The Hayes sisters, they call us, like one collective unit. We all have varying shades of red and reddish-blond hair that our parents must have predicted, probably because my mother and all her siblings have bright red hair. My parents named us Scarlett, Rose, Ginger and Ruby. Scarlett's hair is deep auburn like my mother's, Rose's is copper-colored, Gigi's is reddish-gold with sun-bleached highlights and mine is strawberry blond. We all have unusual, amber-colored eyes—almost yellow in mine and Gi's case—and apparently the kind of looks that get attention. Whenever we walk down the street, people stare. Being eighteen and just released from jail a.k.a boarding school, I've been the least visible, I guess you could say. So I haven't really had a chance to find out about all that. To test it.

And I do: I *feel* like testing it. I want to taste every ounce of my new freedom. I don't plan on wasting a single minute of it and I can't wait to get started.

"You're free!" yells Gigi as I run down the hallway toward my room.

Don't I know it.

I can hear Momma mumble something about getting a job, but that can wait. I've got other plans for the rest of my afternoon.

I get to the bedroom I share with Gi and strip off my worn uniform, shoving it into a bag I plan on burning the very first chance I get.

Rummaging through Gigi's drawers, I can't find what I'm looking for: two pieces that match. God knows I'm not wearing that awful bathing suit they gave us at boarding school, which may as well be a chastity belt. So I go up the back staircase into Rose's room, which she has all to herself now that Scarlett has moved out.

"Rose?" I knock softly. "It's me."

I don't bother waiting for her to answer. She's on her bed, scrolling on her phone. "Hi, Ruby."

A song's playing on her speaker. It's one I've heard before, on the radio when Gi picked me up to go to the clinic a few weeks ago. *You're my wild, wild girl and I know what you like. Let's go for a ride on a hot summer night. Got you in my arms, babe, feels so good and so right. I'll hold you close all the hot summer night.*

Whoever the singer is, he's got a good voice. The tune is equal parts haunting and hot, somehow. It sticks with you in a way you can feel.

Buying myself a phone is priority number one. It's basically cruel and unusual punishment in this day and age to deprive us of something so essential. I'm eighteen years old and I've never in my life had my own phone. Which is ridiculous. Of course we weren't allowed one at school. Phones are windows into the world, luring us to the dark side, of vanity and sin and sex.

Secretly, I can't *wait* to start sinning. "Has he called yet?"

"No. *Asshole.*" Rose's boyfriend is a musician. He's on the road all the time and he doesn't always have time to keep in touch.

My two oldest sisters have a way of inviting a whole lot of drama into their lives. Not me. I've got a plan and I'm sticking to it, no matter what. Daddy used to call me determined and I guess that's one word for it. There's more to it than that, though. They say I'm a dreamer but the thing is, to me my destiny feels like a sure thing. It just does. I know where I'm going and I know exactly what I need to do to get there. I'll make my way to the city, start auditioning and sending out songs. I'll get myself heard by the right people. Everyone says it's too competitive but

I *know* I'm good enough. I can feel the deep pool of my own grit like molten fire, waiting and mixing there, boiling over.

"I'm sure he'll call today." I help myself to Rose's closet, and Scarlett's. "I need a bikini." I finally find a white matching set. Rose is distracted so I strip off and try it on in front of her mirror. It's skimpy as hell—basically three tiny, strategically-placed triangles that barely cover me—but who cares, it's not like anyone's going to see me in it. Then I hold up one of Rose's sundresses. "Can I borrow this?"

"No."

I slip the sundress over my head. "I'll see you a little later. Don't worry about it, Rose. He'll call soon."

"Hey, I said you couldn't—"

"I won't get it dirty," I tell her as I slip out the door.

"Ruby!"

Growing up with three sisters, we argue over clothes all the time. It's not like she hasn't stolen everything I own at least five times.

I head down the stairs and grab my leather bag that has all my music in it. Then I make a bee line for the screen door.

"We need to talk about your summer job, young lady," Momma starts.

"Ruby, there's a letter here from Chase," says Gi.

I go into the kitchen, grab the letter that's sitting on the kitchen table, kiss Momma on the cheek and grab an apple from the fruit bowl. "I'll get a job tomorrow," I tell her. "Today, I'm going for a swim."

"That pond is private property," Momma points out. I'll give her points for consistency. She says that every single time. But no one's lived on the farm next door to ours for as long as I've been away at boarding school. I figure their swimming pond is fair game. Not to mention their piano, but Momma doesn't know about that part.

I head out the back door and across our yard, past the sheds. I climb over the wooden fence and make my way across the field. The rolling hills and the treetops stretch out as far as the eye can see.

It's a beautiful afternoon. Hazy and hot and humid. The kind of day where you can see the dust and the tiny insects, flickering and sun-touched, like lazy unhurried promises floating through the air. As soon as I reach the pond, I peel off my sundress and wade into the sparkling water. It feels amazing on my warm, sweat-dampened skin.

The magnitude of this moment is really starting to sink in. Today is where it all starts. Today's the day I can start making my own rules and following my own road.

Straight to Nashville.

I stand there thigh-deep, splashing cool water onto my arms. Damn, there *really* isn't much to this bikini. I'm spilling out of it. I've filled out over the past year and I'm curvier than I used to be. The minuscule shreds of fabric barely cover the parts they're supposed to cover. If only the nuns could see me now. The thought makes me smile. Sister Louise would have me reciting Hail Marys for an entire week.

Wading further, I let the icy-fresh water rise over my hips. Then I swim out and float there, on my back, appreciating my newfound freedom. It feels so damn good.

The cool, gentle water swirls around me. It's weirdly … *sexy*. Like my solitude and my almost-nakedness are triggering new, lusty tendencies. I float, letting it build. *Damn.* So *this* is what freedom feels like.

I swim back to shore and climb onto the big flat rock that's warm from the sun.

I lay there for a while. It's so damn *liberating* to be alone. To have no one eagle-eyeing you to make sure your virtue is still intact or chaperoning your every move.

The reason they kept us locked away so securely is becoming more obvious with each passing moment. Because I can *feel* myself coming to life, right here under the summer sun. A wildness is taking hold in this perfect blue-sky heat. My body is young and lush. I'm wearing only a few shreds of clothing. I'm wet and hot and fiercely *alive*, maybe for the first time ever. My skin is all sparkly from the water, lit with jeweled diamond-drops.

And I *am* having impure thoughts.

I try not to, but that song keeps playing in my head. The one I heard in the car with Gi. The one that was playing just now in Rose's bedroom. I remember the singer's deep voice with its graveled husk. The memory of that melodic rasp inspires a strange flush on my skin.

You're my wild, wild girl and I know what you like. Let's go for a ride on a hot summer night. Got you in my arms, babe, feels so good and so right. I'll hold you close all the hot summer night.

It makes me think of something Rose told me, whispered late at night the last time I was home. Gi and I were so shocked. Rose said her boyfriend kissed her … *there.*

And then he licked me until … something happened. I can't even describe how good it felt. It's the best feeling I've ever had.

I couldn't *believe* that. It's absolutely the craziest thing I ever heard.

Well, maybe not *ever.* Scarlett used to tell us stuff too. Like how she once … *sucked on her boyfriend's … cock,* she called it, until something happened. Until he *came,* she said. She sort of described what happened until Gi and I were beside ourselves because we'd never heard anything as scandalous as that. Not even close.

Thinking about both of those things now, it makes me feel sort of edgy. Like I'm still blushing at the feelings Rose described.

The heat of the sun seems to center in a particular place. *That* place. Like a slow, curling pulse. I lay still for a while, letting the secret pulse take hold. I think of trying to put it out of my mind, like I should. I think of trying to resist its licking heat. But it's too sweet, this little promise, deep inside my own body.

My hand moves, without me even moving it. I touch my fingers lightly to the place. It feels *good*. I feel ripe, like a sun-sweet peach. Brimming.

I start to move my fingers a little, very gently.

I imagine *his* strong hands, strumming his guitar as he sings that song, like he's singing just for me.

He kissed me and then he licked me until … something happened.

As my fingers barely move, a strange and beautiful thing starts happening to me … a curl of sweet warmth that builds and bursts in a soft pleasure that washes through me, *there*, in a swell of intense, clenching waves. I moan a little. I lay there sort of blissed out for a while as the ripples linger.

Damn. What was that?

When I move again, and sit up, I feel strange. I feel *beautiful*. More beautiful than I can ever remember feeling. Slowly, I stand up. I walk down to the water's edge. Gently, I splash myself. My stomach, my face, my breasts. My nipples, which had softened in the sun-warmth, bud into tight little peaks. Wow. It's *intense*, to be this aware of your own … awakening.

I'm still wet but the house will be an oven so I don't bother drying all the way off. I carefully roll up Rose's dress and put it in my bag. Then I walk up the small incline toward the old farmhouse.

I love this house. It's in need of a paint job and a few repairs but whoever built it must have had some serious money. We don't know exactly what happened to the owners. Maybe they died or moved away and never bothered to sell it. Maybe they thought they'd come back one day.

Either way, it's been a lucky score for me because just inside the huge windows at the front of the house sits the most beautiful grand piano you've ever seen. When I first saw it I couldn't believe my eyes.

I'm not usually the kind of girl who breaks into other people's houses, but I figured it's a terrible waste not to put something so extraordinary to good use. As it turned out I didn't even need to break in. One of the sash windows at the front of the house wasn't locked. All I had to do was slide it up.

It's my favorite way to compose music. You can play your heart out on a guitar but a piano's best for writing, for me at least. I've written all my best songs sitting right here. It felt like whoever moved out of this house left it here just for me. Divine providence or something, that's how I see it.

God, it must be ninety-six in the shade today. I pull the window up. I haven't been here for a while and it's heavy and stuck but I keep trying until I'm finally able to slide it all the way up. It's hotter than hell in the house but the fresh air stirs the sun-flecked dust and I step inside.

I sit on the piano bench and pull my music out of my bag. Chase's letter falls to the floor. I pick it up and open it. Chase and I have been writing letters ever since his family moved to Portland, Oregon three days before my fourteenth birthday. We'd been best friends our whole childhood. We met on the first day of school and ate lunches together and played flashlight tag with my sisters and his two older brothers. When his dad got offered a job on the west coast we both thought our hearts would break. I didn't know how I was going to function without a best friend. We started writing letters because it was the only way we could keep in touch after I went to boarding school. One letter a month for four years is a lot of letters. I've told Chase Lee every secret I've ever had. And even though we haven't seen each other in a long time it's nice to know he's out there somewhere. He always said that someday he'd show up on my doorstep and we'd pick up right where we left off.

Hey Roo,

By now you will have graduated. Free of St. Mary's for good!!! I'm sure it's the best feeling in the world. You little free bird, I wish I could see you and help you celebrate. I'd drive you to Nashville myself.

I've met some new people recently, Roo, in the summer classes I've started at the university here. I'm sharing an apartment with a few of them. You'd like them. They're musicians. There's a funky and thriving music scene here in Portland. You should come and check it out for yourself.

You could stay here, as long as you want. Mi casa es su casa. I have a spare couch in my room (you could have my bed of course). Now that you're free you should really think about it. You wouldn't have to pay rent or anything. I might even be able to get you a waitressing job if you want one.

God, I would love to see you again, Ruby. I say this all the time but I can't believe it's been four whole years. Send me another picture when you get a chance. When are you getting a phone?

Write back to me as soon as you get this. Or even better, call me. I can't wait to talk to you and hopefully I'll see you soon. Please think about coming out here. My graduation gift to you is a bus ticket. Call me!!! I have a new number: 503-320-9218.

Your best friend for life,

C.

Wow.

It's a nice offer.

I think about it for … around half a second.

I slide Chase's letter back into its envelope and stuff it into my bag.

I can't go to Oregon. I mean, I *could*. But I won't. My

heart's been set on Nashville since I was six years old. Since that day when I first picked up my daddy's guitar and started strumming. I sang a song to him and he smiled and said, *honey, one day I'm going to hear you sing at the Grand Ole Opry, mark my words.*

Nashville is my destiny. Nashville is *calling* me. It's been calling me all along.

I take out some of my music. I start to play, and I sing along to a tune I've been working on. I use my pencil to change a couple of the notes and I start again.

Give me everything. I'm on my way. My dreams whispered promises that won't fade away. I want to burn and I want to fly. I don't have it in me not to live and to try.

The song is good enough, I know it is. This one will be my very first single.

I wonder what it'll feel like … to burn and to fly. All those nights as I lay awake in the bunk room of my boarding school, I thought about the long list of things I want to experience, to make my words ring true and not just sound like wistful dreams. To give my songs layers and heart and heat. I write about being on the road, falling in love, feeling the touch of a man—as my sisters have described to me in detail.

It's the best feeling I've ever had.

I want to know that feeling.

Lust and love and … everything that comes with it. *The feel. The taste.*

It's hard to write about things you've never even done.

Heartbreak, even. Loneliness and beauty and road dust on your skin. The rush of singing on stage to a crowd of a thousand people.

All of it.

That's why I'm going to say yes to everything that comes along. Every opportunity. Every dream and every desire.

I sing the last note. As soon as I do, I feel the prickly heated sensation of someone's gaze.

I turn and my heart nearly jumps out of my chest.

I stand up in mute shock, almost knocking over the piano bench.

Someone's here.

A man.

He's been watching me.

His hair is mink-brown but glints with a sun-bleached top layer. He's *big*. Strong-looking. Tall and broad. He's not wearing a shirt. All he's wearing is a pair of worn jeans that hang loose on his lean hips. It vaguely registers behind my panic that he's muscular. Very. Like, *cut*, as Rose would say. I've never seen anyone so outrageously … *masculine* in my life. His skin is sun-bronzed. There are a few tattoos inked to his shoulders and arms. There's a dusting of hair on his chest, which for some reason shocks me. I'm not used to men. He might be in his early twenties or even twenty-five. And even through my alarm I'm aware that he's *insanely* handsome. In an over-the-top kind of way and with a reckless edge, like even though he's gorgeous he could be … dangerous.

We're both stunned in place. He looks as shocked as I feel. There's more to it than that, though. Something darker. *Hungry*, that's how he looks. His eyes drop from my face to my body, lingering on my breasts. To my stomach. Lower. Then back to my face.

God.

I haven't been this close to a man—especially a half-naked one, and *especially* not while wearing what I'm wearing right now—ever.

I'm trespassing. I have no clothes on. And I have no idea what he might do.

It's obvious by his size and his strength that he could do … anything he wanted.

The thought scares me.

I step through the open window.

And I run.

3

———

TRAVIS

Two hours earlier ...

I RUN my hand through my hair and take a swig from my flask. The temperature on the dashboard screen of my Shelby reads 98°.

The countryside is ridiculously picturesque. And I'm *alone.*

It feels so damn good.

The trickle of new ideas swirls somewhere behind my brain. Already.

I don't usually have trouble writing. Or at least I didn't. Until lately. Hell, I was starting to worry that the well of my inspiration had run dry. The music used to come so easily, until I couldn't help but pick up a guitar and start strumming along to it. The urge to write it down and let it out would wake me up in the middle of the night. *Every* night. But lately … there's been nothing. No tunes humming behind my thoughts or notes hanging in the air. None of the lyrics that flit across my mind seem to come together in a way that works. So I've been grappling with the realization that maybe there are only so many songs a person can write before things just fizzle out.

But now, as I cruise along the country road with George Strait cranked up, I can feel the threads of inspiration starting to uncoil.

It's a relief.

And it's exactly what I was hoping for. All I needed was some distance. From the demands of our grueling schedule, the long days and sleepless nights, the band, roadies, photographers, journalists and the chattering endless legions of culture-vultures who all want a slice of yours truly.

I'm even burned out on the fans, if you can believe that. The women pounding on my doors and camping outside my houses. Begging me and my brothers to let them into our lives and our beds. So *many* of them. At first we didn't mind being "God's gift to women, times three"—Rolling Stone's description, not ours. Of course we didn't mind. Most people only dream of the kind of fame and stardom and crazy wealth we've achieved in a few short years. But for all the recognition and devotion, there's something so … *easy—too* easy—about the romantic side of this superstar life. Not that I'm complaining. But they're all so damn *willing*. So easy to please. So ready to give up everything about themselves, in every possible way, in a desperate attempt to get close to you. They'll tell you anything you want to hear. Truth, lies, it doesn't matter. They'll whitewash their lives and their souls for you, if you'll just say yes to them. They only have one thing to give. Turns out it's not enough.

After a while, the one-sided desperation takes the shine off. You start looking for a challenge. Some fire and fury to match your own.

Anyway, I'll show up to our last two shows and sing my heart out. Other than that, over the next few weeks all I want to do is to fully immerse myself in solitude and some undistracted writing time. To be alone with my thoughts. To let the music spool its way out of my fingertips and onto the page, with no interruptions.

My phone rings through the Bluetooth. *Roxie* flashes up on the dashboard screen.

"Hey, Rox."

"Where are you?"

"On my way to my new house."

She pauses at the news. "What new house?"

"The one I bought last night. Out in the country."

"Travis. Why? We're still on tour."

"With two home shows left. I'm only forty minutes out of town. I need some peace, Rox."

"You'll get peace when the tour's over, Travis. I need you in Nashville at nine a.m. tomorrow morning. You have that interview with Alana Powell and Fergus Rollins. All three of you have to be there. *On time*."

Shit. I completely forgot about that. Alana Powell and Fergus Rollins have a popular show on some entertainment network where they interview celebrities. Roxie's been trying to put the interview together for months.

"Please don't tell me you forgot about it."

I don't bother confirming it.

Roxie sighs. "It's going to be impossible enough to get Vaughn there on time. I'm going to have to drive him there myself." I feel for my little sister, trying to manage the three of us. Some days it isn't easy. The stress and manic demands of three months on tour have taken their toll. I sometimes forget she's only 22. My sister is a firecracker but she has her own demons to deal with, some of which overlap with mine, Vaughn's and Kade's, but not all of them. You don't grow up with parents like ours and walk away unscathed. Not that they were *bad* parents, just … complicated ones. Like so many are.

Roxie and Vaughn were always close as kids. Both black-haired and blue-eyed, they've got the look of our father, and the personality too. Stubborn with a passionate edge. While Vaughn gives in to his crazy side, Roxie fights against hers. But they're similar people, both full of life and an energy that burns high and draws people in. Watching Vaughn walk the line of self-destruction is hard on all of us but most of all her.

And so much for hiding myself away.

"Can you please just get here by eight thirty, Travis?"

"You said nine."

"We start at nine fifteen. Try to get here early. I'll text you the address."

"I'll be there." I know I'll regret offering this but I hear myself saying, "And I'll pick up Vaughn."

"You will?"

Knowing my younger brother, he'll be a handful, like he always is. Roxie's got enough to do. "Yeah."

"Thank you so much, Travis. I owe you one."

"You owe me more than one. But I'll let you off this time."

"Love you, Trav."

"Love you too, honey. See you tomorrow." I end the call.

Your destination is on the left.

I slow down and pull into a long driveway. This must be it.

The gravel road gently winds for half a mile or so, with spaced oak trees lining the length of it. There are fenced fields and in the distance I can see a rolling slope overlooking a scenic pond.

The house is spectacular, even if it's in obvious need of a paint job and a few repairs. The landscaping is ragged and the lawn is overgrown. I remember from the listing that it was originally built in the 1850s but was completely refurbished in the 1980s, commissioned by some architect from Atlanta. *A tribute to rustic, authentic Southern charm with a twist of modern farmhouse flair.*

I can't believe my luck, finding this place.

I park behind the enormous barn. When I open the door of my air-conditioned car, the heat of the afternoon hits me like a wall of hot air. I pull my t-shirt over my head and tuck the end of it into my back pocket. Digging into the envelope the real estate office couriered to the warehouse overnight, I fish out a ring of keys. I find the one with the tag labeled *BARN DOOR*. It takes some wrangling but the rusty lock finally clicks open.

I slide the heavy wooden door open and step inside.

Holy shit.

Rays of sunlight spill through a high broken window. Birds chirp from the rafters. The space is huge, almost twice the size of our warehouse in the city. It's ancient and rustic as fuck and has a lonely, old-time atmosphere. There are empty stalls for animals and a ladder leading up to a dusty loft.

Whoever abandoned the property four or five years ago left everything behind. All the old gear and farming equipment is still here—even a rusty and dilapidated pick-up truck, parked in a bay at the far side of the barn.

If someone asked me to describe the ideal location to shoot our next video I couldn't even have dreamed up something this perfect.

I'll think about getting it sound-proofed at some point but we'll keep the rustic feel of it. I take a couple of photos to send to Kade. *Look what I found,* I text him. My brother will love this place.

Fuck, it's hot.

I need a beer.

There are some in my car so I walk back outside.

This place will be my haven. My secret getaway. I'm not inviting a single person here except *maybe* my brothers and sister.

The blue of the sky and the green of the trees is surreal, the colors are so bright. The pond in the distance looks insanely inviting. I'll head down there later to check it out. There's a big smooth plane of rock and even a sandy beach.

And that's when I hear it.

Music.

Someone's playing a piano.

It sounds like it's coming from inside the house.

I find the backdoor and the labeled key on the ring. This time it slides in easily. I open the door and step inside. The kitchen is massive and would have been state-of-the-art five years ago. Whoever used to own this house had good taste and plenty of money.

The music stops for a few seconds.

Then it starts up again.

It's a girl's voice. She's singing as she plays.

I walk down a hallway, toward the music.

I stop at the wide doorway that leads into a spacious

living room, where there's a wall of windows and a grand piano.

And there, sitting at the piano … *holy fuck* … is a girl. She's distracted by her song and unaware of my presence.

At first I think my eyes are playing tricks on me.

She's … *unbelievably gorgeous.*

More than gorgeous. Golden and wet and practically naked. Lit softly by the rays of the sun. Her beauty hits me like a billion-watt lightning bolt, then settles into me, as though I'm cast in an electric trance that has the power to rock your world and make you crazy all at the same fucking time.

All she's wearing is a *very* skimpy bikini.

Holy hell, I mean it. I actually blink a couple times just to make sure I'm not hallucinating. I don't take drugs but Dr. Daniels can stay with you for a while if you overdo the prescription. Not that I drank that much last night. At least I don't think I did.

But … *this.*

Jesus H. Christ.

Her long hair is a very pale shade of red. It hangs to her hips and catches all these vivid hues of the sunlight, like she's iridescent or something. She's sparked with a colorful radiance that's blowing my goddamn mind.

God help me. *Her body.*

She's lush and curvy but at the same time slim and youthful.

Her voice as she sings is bell-pure with a smoky edge.

It's the voice of an angel with a taste for the devil, that's what it is. I don't recognize the song. What I *do* recognize is that she's fucking good, and I wonder for a second if I'm having some kind of religious experience.

An angel lives in the abandoned house I just bought. Is this … real? Am I hallucinating? Have I died and gone to heaven?

She sings the last note.

She feels my presence then, and turns to look at me.

Shocked, with a thread of panic in her expression, she stands up.

I want to tell her not to be scared of me.

But I can't.

Because the combined effect of her *face* and her hair and her lips and her *body—Holy Mother.* Her nipples are luscious little peaks, high on her pert, bouncy breasts. Her hips are flared and feminine, her stomach pale and flaw-less. My cock hardens and throbs. Her tiny, wet bikini is practically see-through. The thin fabric clings tightly to the shape of her ludicrous body. *I can clearly see the outlines of her nipples. Not just the outlines. The color. The shape.* My eyes rove lower. *I can see the lightly plump pinkness of her pussy under the barely-there covering.* My cock gets instantly and fully rock-hard, pressing painfully against the button fly of my jeans.

She's the most beautiful thing I've ever seen.

Ever.

We're locked in this mute, charged staring contest and all I can think is: *I want to lick the dewy sweat from her skin. I want to rip off that tiny bikini and feast on her nipples as I slide my hard cock inside all that snug, wet, golden beauty.* My lust is so fierce it shocks me.

In all my twenty-five years I have *never* seen anything or anyone so entirely … addictive. I'm already fucking hooked.

But then, like she's made of magic, she turns in a sunlit whirl and jumps through the large open window.

No.

I follow her and I can see that she's running across the field, toward a fence. She looks back to see if I'm chasing her. I am. Not *chasing* her, but following her. To the goddamn ends of the earth if I have to. I feel dazed but also laser-focused. I'm not about to lose her. I watch her climb over the fence. In the distance, there's a house.

Her house.

She disappears inside.

What do you know, the little golden songbird is my new neighbor.

Oh, I'll go after her. I almost do it now. I'll break down her door so I can stare at her wet, golden beauty as long as I want. I'll hold her down and lick those soft, parted lips.

Fuck.

Since when do you go around breaking down doors, cowboy?

I don't know why I do it but I collapse onto the grass of the sloping front lawn. I lay there on my back, arms out, looking up at the sky and a few slow-moving clouds.

I'll go to her.

I know where she lives. And I need a minute.

I've just been cursed, that's what this feels like. I'll never *not* have a fucking hard-on again. Every time I think of her, like I am right now, my ten-inch cock will get hot and engorged and thick to the point of spilling pre-cum because I'm almost there already, and if I don't fuck her or jerk off or get drunk I'll go insane.

I'm breathing hard. I unbutton a few buttons to ease the pressure.

The shape of her pink pussy through that transparent fabric, holy Jesus. That smooth, barely-wet skin. That silky, colorful hair. Those full, perfect breasts with their poking-out cherry-ripe nipples.

One detail seems strange about the whole mind-blowing encounter. There wasn't a hint of recognition in her expression. No revelatory moment or oh-my-God-it's-you realization. Almost like she didn't know who I was. I guess that's possible, but it's been a long time since anyone has looked at me like that.

I get up and walk down to the pond. Luckily her distant house is behind the hill from the water's edge, otherwise a pair of binoculars would easily reveal that I'm fully loaded, glistening with the beginnings of a sure thing and so hard I'm jutting out of my unbuttoned jeans. My cock is on overdrive and clearly has no intention of deflating anytime soon. *Not until I've eaten her pink pussy and made her all wet and soft and ready for me.*

Fuck.

I'm seriously about to come.

I strip down to my boxers and dive into the water.

I barely remember to swim.

A Tennessee angel just walked into my life. Golden girl paradise got me all twisted up. Give me summer sunlight, girl, sing me your song. Tennessee angel, I'll follow you til I'm gone.

The tune lands fully formed.

I swim to shore. I stumble up the beach and grab my jeans.

When I get to the house I step through the open window and sit down at the piano. I use one of the scraps of paper the angel left behind and start scrawling down the lyrics, before I lose them. The song unspools itself through my fingers in a rush of funky chords and unexpected melodies.

It's the best thing I've written in a long time. Maybe ever.

Holy hell.

I finish the first song and scribble ideas for two more. The lyrics—for the first time in ages—mesh perfectly with the tunes. By the time I've finished getting it all down, it's dark outside the wall of windows. The moon is full, hanging low in the sky.

I've been sitting here for hours.

There's a dusty lamp next to the piano and I turn it on. The real estate agent must have had the power turned on this morning, like he said he would.

The angel left her bag. And all her music. The song

she sang is still on the piano stand. *Ruby Hayes* is written in the top corner.

Ruby Hayes.

Mine.

The song's title is *Nashville Days*. I play it, humming along to the scrawled lyrics. I can tell from her scribblings and crossed-out notes that she wrote the song herself. I can see the changes she's made are good ones.

She's a talent.

She's a goddess.

And she's made it easy for me.

I pull on my jeans.

Then I put the sheet of music back into her bag and sling it over my shoulder. I step through the open window. The hot night is thick with the chorus of cicadas.

Making my way out to my car, I find myself a clean shirt and I grab my guitar.

Under the light of the full moon, I start walking across the field.

4

"Ruby! There's a phone call for you," Rose yells from the kitchen. "It's Chase."

I've been hiding out in my room since I got back, pacing, strumming my guitar but not having the concentration to play it, *remembering every detail of him.* Gigi's out. She has a four-hour afternoon shift at the library three times a week and I'm glad to have the space to … *absorb* what just happened to me. To process all the adrenaline that's pumping through my veins right now.

My heart's still beating fast. My blood feels hot and my skin is flushed.

God.

I left my music behind. My bag. Rose's dress.

He was so … *hot.* So intense. So big. So … *male.*

"Ruby!"

I pull one of my own sundresses over my head and open my bedroom door. "I'm *coming*."

Our landline is the original phone that was in our house when my parents bought it more than twenty years ago. It has a long cord that reaches around the corner of the kitchen to a chair in the dining room that doesn't entirely allow for private conversations but at least it's out of the kitchen, where Rose and Momma are cooking dinner. I pick up the phone and pull the cord as far as it will go. Outside the window, the sun is low in the sky, starting to set. The sky is tinted orange along the hazy horizon. I can see the roof of the abandoned farmhouse from here.

Not abandoned.

He *lives there.*

With his low-strung jeans on and nothing else. With his big, sweat-glistening muscles and his sun-bleached hair.

"Hi, Chase."

"Hey, Ruby. How are you?"

"Great. Finally finished."

"How does it feel to be free?"

"It feels amazing. "

"Did you get my letter?"

"Yes." *It's in my bag, sitting on his window seat. Will I be brave enough to go back there and confront him and apologize for trespassing and ask for my stuff? I'll* have *to be brave enough. I need to get my music. But what if—*

"Did you think about what I said? About maybe coming out here?"

"It's such a nice offer, Chase, and I'd love to see you but … I got a job." I have no idea why I lie about this. I never lie. I never *need* to lie and I don't know why I'm doing it now. I feel bad about it so I backtrack. "I mean, I *might* have a job. It's not that I don't want to come to Portland, it's just that I—"

"Let me guess. You want to go to Nashville."

My lie didn't work anyway. He knows me too well. "You know that's been my dream all along, Chase. I have to go to Nashville."

"I knew you'd say that, Roo. It's okay. I just really want to see you."

"Maybe you could come here for the summer." But I know he won't. He never comes back. He left all those years ago and he hasn't come back once.

"I wish I could. I'm taking a couple of summer classes at the university here and I have a job. I'm working as a bartender three nights a week."

"It sounds like everything's going really well for you."

"It is. But I miss you, Roo. A lot."

"I miss you too."

"How about coming out for a few days? Or a long weekend? I could pay for it. I could send you a plane ticket."

"That would be so expensive."

"I probably have almost enough. You could come and

spend four or five days with me. Just to check it out in case you change your mind."

"You shouldn't spend your money on that, Chase. You'll need it for school."

"I *want* to spend it on you, Ruby. I want to see you."

I try to gently change the subject. I do want to see him. But I need to focus on my goal of writing and practicing and saving up enough money to get myself to Nashville. Detours will only slow me down at this point. "Are you taking some art classes? Or just accounting?" Chase told me in his letters that he decided to become an accountant. That's what he's studying. I actually tried to talk him out of it. He used to draw a lot and was always daydreaming about becoming an artist.

"No. No art, just accounting. And I know what you're going to say, that it's boring and I'm selling out to go for the stable career over the creative, bohemian lifestyle."

"I wasn't going to say that. It's up to you."

"I'm not doing it only for the money, Roo. I'm doing it for us."

"What do you mean?"

"I want to see you. And *be* with you. I could support you while you write your songs and audition."

"Support me? I won't need that, Chase. I'm going to support myself."

"Sure you will. I know. But what I mean is that I—"

"Dinner's ready, Ruby," calls Momma from the kitchen. Gigi walks in the front door just then and she's got a pail full of peaches she picked up on the way home. So now Momma and Rose and Gigi are in the dining room where I'm trying to talk to Chase, discussing how ripe the peaches are and how they'll make a pie out of them and how Rose's boyfriend finally called and he's taking her out tomorrow night.

But I'm almost relieved by the interruption. I think Chase is working around to something I'm not sure I'm ready to commit to. I mean, I haven't seen him in *four years*. It's too long. Too much has happened to me since then to know how to feel. And I'm right on the cusp of discovering *myself*. I don't know if I have room for checking out Portland, which might as well be Mars at this point since I have zero desire to live there or even visit. There's only one place I really want to be.

Nashville may not turn out to be exactly what I've been dreaming about all these years and I'm okay with that. But it's up to me to figure that out for myself and, come hell or high water, it's where I'm heading.

"Chase. I have to go. I'll think about what you said and we'll talk again soon, okay?"

"I'll call you tomorrow."

I don't mention I'll be job-hunting tomorrow. I told him I had a job. This whole conversation has me confused and sort of angsty about my emotions. I shouldn't be lying to my best friend. I don't have to make excuses. "If I'm out, leave a message." We have one of those archaic old answering machines but it still works.

"One of these days we're going to figure out how to get together again, Ruby. And soon."

"Of course we will."

"Did you get your phone yet?"

"Not yet."

"As soon as you do we can talk all the time and message each other."

"Yeah. I can't wait."

"I love you, Roo. I'll call you tomorrow."

"Love you too. Bye."

We eat dinner and Rose is in one of her rare good moods because her boyfriend finally called and he's going to be in town tomorrow so he said he'll take her out to dinner. We all go into the den to watch some show on Netflix but I don't feel like watching TV. Besides, I've missed the first three episodes of whatever they're watching so I go into my room and sit in the chair by my window and pick up my daddy's old guitar.

I *am* brave enough to go back to the house. Those are my only copies of some of those songs. I'll just apologize for breaking in. *But ... is it safe? What if he's dangerous? Or angry?*

He didn't look angry. He looked ... *dazzling. Muscular. Sweaty.*

I try not to think about it.

That dusting of dark hair on his chest. His defined abs and the loose fit of his worn jeans.

I stare out the window at his house in the distance. As I do, a low light turns on.

What's he doing now? Is he alone?

I strum a few chords, then I put my guitar down and I turn out my light. I lay in bed and I can see the glow of the lamp in his window from here.

The fascinating strength of his big, hard, masculine body.

The dark look in his eyes, like he was thinking … very dirty thoughts.

A while later Gigi comes in. She tells me a little about the ending of the show they just watched. Then she says goodnight and goes to bed. I try to sleep.

I can't.

After a few minutes, I hear Gigi's soft, even breathing from the other side of the room.

I didn't tell her.

I'm not sure why I kept it to myself. Usually I tell Gigi everything. My sister knows practically every thought I've ever had.

But this feels different. Overwhelming and new. It would be hard to even describe the way he stared at me. The way we stared at *each other.* His crazy appeal and that edge of … something else.

Hunger.

Danger.

Lust.

The very reason I've been hidden in a locked-up school with a very high fence for four years. Even in the summers, we had to do chaperoned community service, garden, study and pray. To shield us from exactly what happened to me today.

But I'm not locked up anymore.

His eyes, so riveted. His wind-blown hair with the ends bleached gold by the sun. *The line of dark hair that disappeared under his button fly…*

It's honestly not something I've ever thought about before, how men are *built* so differently to women. How fascinating those differences are. I wish I could have stared at him a little longer.

What's even more fascinating is that a five-second glimpse of a shirtless red-blooded man can make you feel … thirsty. *To taste.*

God.

Ruby.

Stop.

Those kind of thoughts will only get me into trouble.

But my shame at being caught wet and practically naked in his house today has softened into something else altogether. The sun-touched memory of that lusty, animal look in his eyes makes me squirm under my sheets. I quietly kick the sheet off. It's so hot tonight. I wish I could take off my cotton nightgown and lay naked in the moonlight.

Which is crazy.

And that's not all. I feel that low pulse begin to gently

throb, like it did earlier this afternoon. That awakening sweet heat.

Outside the window, the moon glows full, shining its silver light onto the walls of our bedroom.

At first I almost think I'm imagining it then: a gentle strumming sound, floating in from outside the window.

I look over at Gi but she's curled up, facing the far wall, fast asleep.

And I can't resist. I go to the window and look out.

I stare at him for a few seconds.

It can't be.

But it is.

It's him.

He's sitting on the old bench under the oak tree, strumming his guitar. The night is so bright I can see the dark tan of his skin against the faded yellow of his t-shirt. The fabric is tight over the muscles of his arms as he plays softly. The room I share with Gigi is on the first floor and looks out onto the porch. My mother's and sisters' rooms are upstairs, on the other side of the house, so this soft, gentle strum is unlikely to wake them.

I hope.

I don't want them to see him, or hear him. I want to keep him all to myself.

His hair flicks against the back of his neck and around his ears. His neck is strong-looking, corded and brown. His arms are gently muscled. *I've seen him without a shirt.* Broad and tanned and dusted with hair. Now, his shirt sort of clings to him in the hot night. I can see the sculpted shape of his shoulders and the hard surface of his chest.

I wish I could *touch* him. To feel how hard those biceps are. To play those textures under my fingertips, all that corded, sinewy hardness, so new to me.

He looks up. He sees me. His strumming slows.

I watch him through the thin veil of the screen at my window.

"Hey," he says, still strumming gently. He's cool and unassumingly confident and I can feel that masculine arrogance settle into me like a warm, stealthy physical force.

"Gigi's asleep," I say quietly, just in case he's here for her, even though I'm pretty sure he might be here for me. But I'm new at this stuff.

He continues to strum quietly. "Who's Gigi?"

"My sister. That's who the last one came to sing to."

He laughs softly at this. "Well, I'm not here to sing to Gigi."

I don't reply, but my heart starts beating faster.

"You didn't need to run. I'm not going to hurt you."

I guess it's nice to have that assurance even if I can't be sure it's true. He *could* hurt me or hold me down or do anything he wanted. Weirdly, that detail excites some deep-buried feminine instinct. His obvious brute, masculine power is one of the most alluring things that's ever happened to me, go figure. "Did you buy that house?" I say quietly, thankful that Gigi is a deep sleeper.

"Yeah. Just yesterday. Come outside and sit with me. I want to talk to you about something." His accent is just the faintest bit different. I can't quite put my finger on why, but he sounds ... sophisticated. Like he's picked up on some unknowable wide-world influences. His voice is deep and has a rasp to it. A graveled edge that reminds me of something I can't immediately place and makes the tiny hairs on my arms stand up a little. Not with fear, but something else. Longing, maybe. Wild curiosity.

"I can't."

He strums again, soft and slow. "Why not?"

"I'm ... not supposed to."

To this, he smiles. Not a full smile, just a barely-there half-smile that touches his eyes. Butterflies erupt into flight inside my stomach. The brief flash of his teeth glows white against the dark tan of his face. His hotness is romantic and extreme in the moonlight. Intense and spellbinding. *I want more of it.*

"You always follow the rules," he drawls as a statement, not a question, like he finds this funny.

"Sometimes." It's true, I usually do. You can get detention for a week if you don't follow every instruction the nuns give. I don't even want to think of how my confession would be received tonight if I had to admit what I'm thinking about right now.

But I'm done with all that. I don't have to answer to

other people anymore. I don't have to censor every thought and every desire. This is my youth and my new life. I'm a free woman now.

And this—this *man*—makes me want to break *all* the rules. That cool, cocky jaunt to his manner and his thick hair that barely curls in a way only a man's hair could … it makes me want to do something reckless. It makes me want to do what *he* tells me to do.

"I want to talk to you. About somethin' important."

Through that slight tone of sophistication, there it is: a hometown drawl. Something about the way he drops his g like hot molasses makes me think about his mouth. *The way his lips might taste.*

"Don't be scared of me, Ruby Hayes."

"How do you know my name?"

I notice then that my bag is sitting next to him on the bench. "You wrote it on the song you were singing today."

My face gets hot at the thought of *me singing today.* Wet. Almost naked. *Still euphoric from those waves of pleasure that happened when I … did what I did.*

Getting closer to him will be dangerous. Of course it will. I can feel that already. There's something about him that's almost unbearably enticing. It scares me a little how much I want to give him, already.

"I'm Travis."

"Travis," I whisper before I can stop myself. Another slow flicker of a smile, another strum. He's watching me like he's waiting for a reaction of some kind. I'm not sure what he's expecting. "What did you want to talk to me about?"

"Come out here and I'll tell you. No one'll mind if you come on out and talk to your new neighbor for a minute or two, will they?"

He seems young to be buying his own farm. Especially one that's a hundred acres and probably worth millions. "I guess not."

There's no harm in talking.

I know, though—I *know*—that even *talking* to him will be riskily tempting. His draw is like the coolness of the water on a hot summer day. I can tell just by looking at him that something about him will be impossible to resist. The bronzed skin of his arms that are hair-roughened and warm-looking. You can just tell he'll smell good. Like hay and heat and lust. Already, I know it.

He wants to talk, that's all.

Carefully, as quietly as I can, I raise the screen. I glance over and see that Gigi is still fast asleep. So I crawl through the window and walk barefoot across the porch, down our front steps to where he's sitting under the oak tree. It's only then that I realize my nightie is short and maybe a little sheer in the bright moonlight. It's pink with little white hearts on it. Childish, probably, and almost too small for me now but it's too late to do anything about it.

Besides, he's already seen me in my bikini, which was a lot more revealing than this is.

He's watching me.

I can see the color of his eyes as I draw closer.

Green as spring grass. Shards of it glow neon, they're so bright, like those signs in bars you see as you drive past.

I feel each heartbeat. I'm bridging the divide. My body feels heavy and light at the same time. Heavy with a new, warm femininity, light with anticipation. The glow that began today at the pond is deeper now. Settling into my mouth, my heart, my thighs, the low pit of my stomach.

I stand next to the bench where he's sitting and he stops strumming his guitar. His eyes are on my body, searing me with his emerald-hued awareness. My nipples bud. The hollow between my legs feels warm and soft. My panties cling lightly as I sit on the bench's far end. I don't want to get too close to him. I'm afraid of what might happen.

He looks bigger up close. With his sun-touched looks and broad-shouldered brawn, he reminds me that I need to be careful. I don't know him. I don't know who he is or what he might do. There are veins under the skin of his arms and hands that amplify the promise of his raw strength. If he wanted to, he could overpower me so easily. *He could hold me down. He could pin me under his weight.*

"I liked your song," he says, watching me with lazy contemplation.

A fresh wave of heat rises to my cheeks. "You did?"

"Yeah." His voice is just about the sexiest thing I've

ever heard in my life. Rasped with notes of dark promise and hot lust.

"I … I didn't think anyone was there. I'm sorry I broke into your house. We don't have a piano and I … I've been using yours for a long time."

"You can use it anytime you want."

"Thanks." That's nice of him.

"You ever play for anyone?"

"What do you mean?"

"On stage."

"No. But I will soon enough. Just as soon as I can get to Nashville."

"Nashville." He says it slowly as he strums C, not as a question.

"Yes."

"What's in Nashville?" There's a thread of curiosity in his voice, like he's dying to know.

I know what it'll sound like. The endless procession of wannabes that flock to Nashville, hoping for a miracle, searching for their lucky break. Most of them will never find it. And even though I'm a little self-conscious about what I might look like to him—like one more dreamer in a vast sea of dreamers—I don't care. So it comes out sounding sort of defiant. "My future."

He hears it, and he smiles. "Sing me that song again."

His accent has deepened, and so has mine. "No."

"Go on." He starts strumming my tune and he looks

over at me from under the lush fall of his hair. He's absolutely gorgeous.

It's pretty interesting when you think about it, that a million lessons about temptation never taught me a thing. Now, I finally understand it.

Travis starts playing my song perfectly and it surprises me, that he knows the chords.

"How'd you learn it so quick?"

He smiles and barely shrugs but he doesn't answer my question. "Go on." He plays the opening chords again and I do it. I sing softly along with the tune as he strums it like he's been playing it for years. As I sing, the music, like it always does, inhabits me in a way that takes over and makes me feel better than I do when I'm not singing. The notes weave themselves around the warm night air. It sounds good with him playing it and me singing along. His music, like mine, feels effortless. In this, we're already kindred spirits.

When I've finished the song, I stop.

Travis is quiet for a few seconds. Then he sits back and lets his muscled arms cradle his guitar. I feel a weird sense of jealousy or something like it. I want to know what those arms feel like, warm and strong and carefully possessive. Slung casually with all their powerful promise, around *me*.

"You're good," he says.

"Thanks. You are too. Do you sing?"

His green eyes spangle. "A little. I wrote a song today. You want to hear it?"

"Okay."

He starts playing a tune and as he sings along to it, I can't *believe* how good he is. His voice is deep and again reminds me of something elusive. I can't quite recall what it might be because I'm too lost in the lyrics as he's singing them to me. About a Tennessee angel. I get this odd hunch that the song is about me—but it can't be. He only saw me once, a few hours ago. I know for sure he must be singing about someone else. The song ends and the night feels empty without the husky sway of his voice.

"Wow. You're so good," I tell him, sort of awed by him, for a lot of different reasons.

"Thanks."

"Have you ever thought about making a record?"

That lazy grin. He studies my expression for a few seconds with that searching curiosity again, like I've entertained him in some way. But he doesn't answer my question. Instead, he asks, "What kind of music do you listen to? Who are your favorite artists?"

"Old school ones, mainly. I listen to my daddy's old vinyl collection when I'm home. I don't … well … it's sort of embarrassing but I haven't listened to much new music at all. I've been at boarding school and they never let us listen to anything except hymns."

"Really? Shit."

"Yeah. But I graduated yesterday so as soon as I can

I'm going to listen to everything I can get my hands on and start building my playlist. My sister Rose said she'll show me how. Once I get my phone, that is. I can hardly wait."

A playful smile plays at the corner of his beautiful mouth. "You don't have a phone?"

"No. Not my own. Not yet. But that's the first thing I'm going to buy."

"When are you going to Nashville?"

"As soon as I've earned enough to get myself a place in the city. Something small, it doesn't matter. Then I'll start auditioning. I've got a list of places to try." I don't know why I'm telling him all this. It all sounds more like wishful thinking than anything close to reality. But Travis blinks his thick lashes, watching me with smug amusement and … a beguiled, hot fascination. His gaze is on my parted lips as I speak. I bite my lip and he watches my teeth as they sink gently into tender flesh.

His mesmerizing allure and also his nearness is affecting me in crazy ways. I can feel that warm pulse again between my legs. My panties feel … *wet.* I try to fold my arms since my nipples are poking against the thin cotton of my nightie, but when I do this the short skirt rides further up my thighs.

"You got a list of places to audition, do you?"

"Yes." As gorgeous as he is, his slightly-mocking arrogance riles me a little. A light petulance has crept into my tone. He can mock me all he wants. I'll show him, just like I'll show everybody else. "Anyway, what is it you wanted to talk to me about?"

His green gaze holds mine. "I want you to come and play my piano again. Tomorrow."

It's a very tempting offer. But my goal is rock solid. And it requires money. "I have to look for a job tomorrow. So I probably won't have time. But thanks for bringing my bag back to me."

"What kind of job?"

"Anything that pays real money."

He contemplates me for a few seconds. "I'm looking to hire someone."

"You are?"

"Yeah. I am."

"To do what?"

Travis thinks about this for a few seconds as he watches my eyes. "To play my piano. It's dusty. It needs some use."

He might be teasing me. "That's not a job."

"It is. Have you seen how dusty that thing is?"

"You want … a cleaner?"

"Yeah. A piano cleaner. I was planning on playing it tomorrow afternoon but I've got somewhere I need to be in the morning. You could dust it off for me so it's ready when I get back."

I can tell he's just trying to be nice, maybe. "I need a job that's going to last all summer."

He strums a chord, very gently, still watching my face.

"That's what I'm offering. I want my piano played every day. They sound better when they get used regularly. It warms up the strings. Gives them a better tone."

This almost makes me smile and I roll my eyes, not exactly meaning to. "I don't think that's true."

"It *is* true. Dust dulls the clarity of the sound."

Even if he is just trying to be nice, his offer sure does sound a lot better than working as a waitress, like Rose does, which she hates because she's always getting hit on. Or at the library, like Gigi does, which sounds boring as hell to me. I've spent enough time in quiet buildings where no one's allowed to talk to each other to last me a lifetime.

I could make it worth his while. "I could clean your house for you, if you wanted. I could dust everything and shine the windows and mop the floors too."

"I kind of like it as it is. I like the feel of it."

Regardless, the place needs cleaning. "I could weed the garden and paint the fence too. But I really do have to save up some money this summer so it would depend on how much—"

"I pay a hundred dollars an hour." He's still playing my song, better than *I* could even play it, I can't help noticing.

But then it registers. "A *hundred?*" Is this a joke? A proposition? A—

"You can work as many hours as you want. A full day, every day. Or more. Or less. Whatever you want. Starting tomorrow. And if you want to take days off to do auditions whenever you need to, you can do that too."

I don't know him. What I do know is that this offer is too good to be true.

It's also too good to refuse.

I *should* refuse. As amazing as all that sounds, working for him will be dangerously … tempting. He knows this too. He's smiling that lazy smile, *challenging* me to refuse him. He's so arrogant about it, I almost don't want to give him the satisfaction. "I suppose I could."

"You suppose you could." His smile reaches his bottle-green eyes with their dense lashes and they crinkle around the edges in a way that makes my stomach do a funny little flip. He really is stunning. He leans a little closer and his smile turns wolfish. The look in his eyes is almost daunting, like he wants to eat me alive.

I wish he would. I wish he'd touch me, and cross a line.

"Is that a yes?" His voice is even more husky than before.

I shouldn't really even consider this. He's making *up* a job, just for me, I'm almost sure of it. Why? I mean … I *know* why, and I'll probably accept for the very same reason. I'm too inexperienced to know for sure, but what I do know is that this summer is going to enlighten me in more ways than one, I can feel it already.

You're my wild, wild girl and I know what you like. Let's go for a ride on a hot summer night. Got you in my arms, babe, feels so good and so right. I'll hold you close all the hot summer night.

Chase kissed me once. My only kiss, when I was four-teen years old. The barely-there brush of his lips against mine before he left for the west coast four years ago. At the time, it was the most important thing that had ever happened to me.

Why is it that boys—and now men—make you feel that way? Why is it that the emotions or hormones or whatever it is *they* stir up give the highest highs of all, making everything else seem monotone and dull in comparison? Biology is serious stuff. Preached boundaries don't stand a chance against animal urges, is what I'm learning.

Chase used to joke that we'd get married when we were older. He used to say that we're each other's destiny. I think he was trying to talk about that to me today, actu-ally, when I avoided the subject or we got interrupted.

But Chase isn't here. He hasn't been here for a long time. And he's not where I'm going.

Besides, a job is a job. *A hundred dollars an hour* is a *lot* of money. It's a bribe, maybe. A lure. But it'll get me to Nashville a lot faster than waitressing. There's no way I'd get more than minimum wage at any other job in town.

Anyway, I guess you don't go around buying multi-million dollar farms unless you're financially secure, so he must be able to afford to pay his cleaners very well. Maybe it's a city thing, or wherever he comes from. Now that I look a little more closely, the guitar he's holding is a nice one. One of those expensive ones, with fancy-looking detailing.

I can handle whatever's going to happen. I *have* to handle it. That's what this real world—which is far better than the imprisoned one—is all about. It's time for me to cowgirl up and do what needs to be done.

"All right," I hear myself say. "I'll start tomorrow."

He smiles and it's honestly amazing to me how he's just broken the shackles of four years of indoctrination with one sexy, genuine smile that touches my heart and at the same time makes my thighs sort of tingle. "Good. I have to leave early but you can let yourself in." His gaze lingers on my mouth, almost like he's thinking about kissing me. A pang of longing surges through me. And even though I try to think pure thoughts, all I can do is wonder what his wicked mouth, with those perfect lips, would *feel* like against mine. If he'd be gentle. *Or if he'd be rough.*

Damn it. I'm blushing again.

But I'm too high on this new freedom and the warm effect of his closeness to feel scared or shy or as careful as maybe I should. His big, hard *maleness* is blowing my mind. The dangerous promise of what he could do with all those hard muscles is scaring me and alighting a small, provoked thrill in me all at the same time. There's a bead of sweat at the base of his throat. I want to *lick* him there like I've never wanted anything in my life. I want it so bad I almost do it.

"We can go for a swim when I get back," he says. "After you play me the songs you've been working on."

It's probably a bad idea.

It's *definitely* a *very* bad idea.

You're not locked up anymore, girl, I remind myself again. *This is what freedom is. Live your life. Take your chances and experience things you were put on this earth to find out about. You'll never write a good song if you don't know what any of the stuff you're writing about actually* feels *like.*

He leans closer. I can smell him and it's better than I ever imagined: all hot sun and leather-and-whiskey and man-spiced sin. "You know you want to, darlin'," he murmurs.

Just this near-touch of his mouth is the most erotic experience I've ever had in my life. My lips part. My nipples are tight and painfully sensitive.

Kiss me. Bite me.

But he pulls away.

He stands up and slings the guitar strap over his shoulder. I can only stare at the size of him. He's tall and broad and magnificent in his jeans and faded yellow t-shirt, his hair falling across his forehead in silky layers.

"See you tomorrow, Ruby."

I watch as he walks off into the night humming the song I sang to him, his jeans hugging his body in ways I can't even explain and I'm reeling from the realization that, just like that, everything has changed.

I don't know how or why or what any of it means.

But I'm pretty sure I'm about to find out.

5

TRAVIS

Don't turn around.

Don't turn around.

Do. Not. Look. Back.

I know for sure that if I turn to see her sitting there on the bench in her tiny, see-through dress, I'll go to her, sling her over my shoulder and carry her away with me. Kicking, screaming, I wouldn't care.

I'm not a deviant. Not usually, at least. I'm a mostly-wholesome, hot-blooded, down-home country boy who helps old ladies cross the street and gives shitloads of money to charity.

But *this girl.*

She could drive me to do things I would never in a million years have considered before I saw her sitting there playing my piano all soft and wet in the warm sun. I want to steal her.

Not only that, but I want to devour her. I want to dirty her purity with my hot cum until she's all sticky and slick and covered in it. I want to fuck her hard and slow until she's crying my name. Until my seed is spilling out of her and dripping down her thighs.

Sweet Jesus.

I need to calm the fuck down.

I need to get my bearings and let her come to me. Tomorrow. She'll be there waiting for me when I get back from the interview.

And if I thought I was fucked *before* she tip-toed out her window to sit next to me on the old bench under her oak tree, well, now I'm fucking *fucked*.

The moon lit her long hair in ribbons of pale reddish gold. She's all golden freckles and moonglow magic, with lips shaped like a perfect kiss. Her skin is smooth and lightly tanned, so flawless she doesn't look real. And when she smiles it actually feels painful, like my heart is breaking or some crazy shit. Lust, I'll call it, even though that doesn't even come close to describing the blooming magnitude of what's coursing through my veins right now. Obsession, maybe, because I'm agonizingly hard and hot and all twisted up with a need that feels rabid and more savage than anything I've ever experienced in my life.

It took every ounce of willpower I possess and then some not to taste nirvana. Not to lean in and plunge my tongue into her untouched mouth.

She's curious but ridiculously naïve. Her lips are moist

and parted. Her pussy is wet, under her sheer little dress in the moonlight.

She was waiting for a light, sweet kiss.

That's something I can't give her.

I'd have ended up ripping that skimpy, see-through nightgown all the way off. I could see the plush silhouette of her ludicrously-succulent body, her full breasts poking against the soft veil of her dress. If I'd kissed her lips I wouldn't have been able to stop until I'd tasted every inch of her. Until I'd sucked on those high, taut nipples until she squealed, and licked my way down to her damp, clinging panties, ripping them off so I could slide my tongue inside, getting her soft and ready for me.

I would have been *way* too hungry. It's best to wait until we're alone.

I only hope I can go slow enough.

Thank fuck I had the guitar to hold on my lap. My stomach is slick with pre-cum. I'm riding a high, cresting a swell every time I'm near her. It's a fucking problem.

And when she started *singing*, again, it felt like I'd died and was singing alongside an angel in heaven.

Only one detail separates her from absolute purity. It's that taste for more. She's innocent but she's *hot*. Wet. *Almost* ready. Her light reticence is underscored with sweet, untried curiosity.

Holy hell.

Her bell-toned voice has a light, smoky rasp that gives her innocence a raw, lust-fringed undertone. The angelic clarity will get her noticed. But it's that gentle husk that will make her a superstar. There's depth there, a hint of untouched wildness she doesn't even know about yet. But I do. I can hear it. I can *taste* it. And it's *that* detail about my little Tennessee angel that has me more worked up than any other.

She's got a hunger in her eyes I recognize. It's the same hunger *I* used to have. I still do to a certain extent but when you reach the top it changes. The desperation doesn't feel quite so acute. You begin to take things for granted. Ruby Hayes's starry-eyed passion reminds me of how I *used* to feel. Single-minded and focused on digging into your talent with everything you've got.

It's refreshing. To bask in the warmth of her fire. To watch the little pout of her determination. All that, combined with her obvious talent, it'll be enough. You can see the X-factor radiating off of her along with her stardust and her sweet-hot beauty. My girl looks like fire-works *feel* and there's no coming back from that. There's a heart-pumping, earth-moving power to her presence that makes me realize, already, that she's ruining me for anyone else.

I don't know if I *want* to be ruined for anyone else.

I don't.

I'm not.

You are.

You one hundred percent are. Not one of that endless, faceless procession of adoring worshippers sparked one millionth of the need that's boiling in your blood right now and making you harder than newly-forged steel.

I've already decided that I'm going to make it happen for her.

But not yet.

She's mine. I found her. And I want her all to myself.

The ferocity of my possessiveness is an entirely new supernova exploding into my life at this precise moment.

I'm going to feast on her innocence like a ripe, juicy peach and taste her honey all over my tongue. I'm going to rub my cum all over those full, bouncy, cherry-tipped breasts, those smooth thighs, that softly-plump, pink, wet pussy. I'm going to show her what heaven feels like until she's begging me to come inside her. Until she can't get enough of me because I make her feel so damn good.

Until she's addicted to me and everything I can do.

Hell.

Slow way the fuck down, son. You're horny as fuck on a hot night and need to get laid, that's all. Chill. Take a deep breath and calm down.

Until she's too in love with me to ever leave me.

What the hell's happening here?

Goddamn it.

I PUNCH in the code to open the door to Vaughn's apartment and let myself in. I glance around. The place is an unholy mess, with bottles everywhere, pizza boxes, rolled up dollar bills on the table, overflowing ash trays and people crashed out on every chair and couch in the room. The stereo system is still cranked up.

I'm not in the mood for this shit.

I didn't sleep at all last night. I might have had two hours, maybe less.

When I got back to the house after visiting Ruby, I drank too much whiskey and wrote three more songs. Turns out it's an interesting way to write: with a raging fucking hard-on. That's the good thing about song lyrics. Your spin can be positively filthy but the words only hint at the depth of your goddamn lust.

All the songs are about her. Of course they are.

Her effect has opened the floodgates of my mind, somehow. I couldn't write it all down fast enough.

That's not the only floodgate she's opened. I needed relief. It came—many times—but it didn't last. I woke up on the couch this morning, whiskey bottle still in one hand with my jeans undone and cum all over myself.

I found a shower and cleaned myself up, but I'm on edge. I feel feverish and half-insane.

I pound on Vaughn's bedroom door. "Vaughn. Get up. We have an interview in half an hour." I bang again.

A low groan.

"Answer the door or I'm coming in."

"Fuck off, Travis."

"There's no chance of me fucking off, Vaughn. Get

up or I'm coming in, I mean it. Roxie's been working on this for months. I don't want to do it either but I'm here, showing up." That's me, the reliable one, the easy-going one, the stable one. Except that right now I feel less stable than I ever have. "Let's just get it the fuck over with."

Nothing.

I bang again.

"Leave me alone," he groans. "I need sleep."

I open the door. Vaughn's in bed and there are two girls in bed with him, barely covered with a sheet.

"What the *fuck*, Travis?" My brother's black hair is wild and his eyes are ridiculously bloodshot.

"Get up and take a shower," I tell him. "I don't really want to fight with you or drag you out myself, so just do it. Without the drama."

He glares at me. "Where have you been? Kade was looking for you last night. You weren't answering your phone."

I glare back at him. "I bought a house."

"Another one?"

"Yeah."

"Where?"

"Outside Nashville. Out in the country."

"No shit."

"I'll show it to you later." Maybe it'll be enough. If I drag him out of this non-stop bender, maybe he'll be able to take a step back from his own self-destruction. My brother has never been good at saying no. Everyone wants to hang out with him because he's always the life of the party, to say the least, but if he could just get some space he might be able to gain some perspective and see how out of control he is.

He climbs out of bed, keeping the sheet wrapped around his waist. Which means he pulls it off of the two naked girls, who squeal in protest.

"You've got ten minutes," I tell Vaughn, ignoring the girls.

He slams the bathroom door.

The girls pick their clothes up off the floor and partially cover themselves. "Hi, Travis," one of them smiles at me coyly.

Seriously?

I walk out and go into Vaughn's shamble of a kitchen to try to find some coffee. I was running late this morning and floored it all the way into the city.

I manage to find some coffee and figure out how the espresso machine works, making two double shots. By the time it's brewed Vaughn is out of the shower, dressed in jeans and a black t-shirt that shows off his muscles and his ink. He's got a few new ones.

The dark circles under his eyes are so bruised-looking they look like shiners and he hasn't shaved but at least he's relatively clean. I hand him his coffee. "Let's go."

Vaughn follows me down to my Shelby and we drive over to the address Roxie gave me, of the studio where we're being interviewed. "Where's the new house?" he asks.

I describe the route. "There's a stone Civil War-era wall that borders the east wall of the property, like a landmark, just before you get to the turn off." I hand him my phone so he can scroll through the photos I took. "Check out the barn."

"This looks amazing." I'll take encouragement from that. Maybe I really can convince him to take some time out.

Roxie looks wildly relieved when we walk in. "I said get here *early*. It's nine fifteen on the dot."

"At least we made it," I say, and she stands on her toes to kiss my cheek, whispering *thank you*.

To Vaughn: "You look like shit." He picks Roxie up in a bearhug and twirls her around. "Put me down!" she squeals. "You smell like someone dipped your Irish Spring in Jack Daniels."

"But you love me anyway." Vaughn sets her on her feet and she introduces us to Alana and Fergus. We start recording and they ask us the usual questions about how we got our start and how does it feel to have so many number one hits and has the fame changed our lives and blah blah blah. I'm over it. Why do none of them—even the so-called successful ones—even attempt to shake up the playbook every now and then?

Vaughn is talkative and funny, probably because he's still drunk. But it's a good thing because I'm distracted and Kade hardly says a word. That scheming little rich chick he's been seeing has obviously barnacled herself onto him in a way that's new. I overheard someone say she's some kind of heiress which explains the bitchy, entitled vibe she gives off. Another reason I'm glad I bought the new house. Both my brothers need a getaway as much as I do.

But not yet. Not today.

I'm in a terrible mood. Partly because I'm here and also because I can't stop revisiting the moonlit curves of a certain angelic little neighbor's crazy-as-fuck body in excruciating detail like a video replay in my head that won't stop. I want to see her. But I don't *want* to want to see her as desperately as I fucking do. She's probably playing my piano as we speak. *Maybe she's wearing her bikini. Maybe she went for a swim and she's all wet and—*

"Travis?"

"What?"

"I asked if your fame has had an impact on your relationships … if you *have* a current relationship," Alana's asking me. "Are you dating anyone right now, in other words." She's extremely groomed-looking, in an uptight, citified way, with short dark hair and a flouncy dress. She's blinking at me like they all do. With a carnal longing that's more than a little lewd. Women melt under my gaze like butter and this one's no different.

"We're here to talk about the music." I grin at her not because I'm friendly but because I just realized she's banging Fergus, whose face is getting red because his secret lover is lusting after the lead singer of her favorite band. Alana glances at him and blushes despite all her attempts not to.

But she's a New Yorker. They don't have manners. "Your fans are dying to know if there's a special certain someone in your life right now. Who are you dating? Our sources tell us you didn't sleep at either of your Nashville properties last night. Who were you with? We want details."

As if I'd tell you about the girl at my piano. She's sweet as fuck, ready for an adventure and she's about to be taken on the ride of her life, as soon as I can get the fuck out of here. There's an edge to my voice that's new, go figure. "There are a lot of special certain someones in my life. A hundred thousand, every night."

Vaughn lights a cigarette. Alana ignores this, even though smoking is obviously not allowed in the studio. Fergus glances up at the sprinkler system that's set into the ceiling.

"*I* have a relationship right now," Vaughn drawls. "Actually two. Ask me."

Alana takes the bait excitedly. "You're *dating* someone, Vaughn? Do tell."

He exhales a smoke ring. "'Dating' is probably over-stating it. But I'm considering calling back these two girls I fucked last night. Damn, those girls could do the most amazing things with their—"

"This show is nationally syndicated," blurts Fergus, in a huff. To some minion standing out of shot, "Edit that out."

Alana is undeterred. "What about you, Kade?"

"No." Pissed off. Like he knows the lie will be received badly by the barnacle, who might even be listening from a nearby waiting room. He looks that tense.

"Kade, there was a photo of you with a … " Alana leafs through her notes. " … an heiress named—"

Roxie interrupts from the sidelines. "It's actually in our contract not to discuss the band's private lives. We agreed on that." She's still glaring at Vaughn. We're supposed to toe the line and behave in polite company.

"Oh, *fine*." Alana turns to me. "So, then, tell us about the meaning of the song Hot Summer Night. You wrote that one, right, Travis? I *love* that song so much. It's one of my all time favorites. Who was it written about? Anyone in particular?"

"Not really. It was a hopeful song. A song I wrote about a phantom lover I was hoping might one day show up."

"*Swoon*," Alana gushes, but I tune her out.

Because maybe she just *has* shown up.

Don't overreact, for fuck's sake. You met her once. Twice. For a total of twenty minutes. You can't know that fast. It's lust, pure and simple. A raging, diabolically intense lust, yes, but nothing more. Get it out of your system and move on.

I keep it light. I go through the motions, even though my head is spinning. I make shit up. Like I always do.

But I don't feel like toeing the line. Not at all. In fact, I don't think I can do this anymore.

I'm trying not to continuously retrace in my mind the outline of her sweet pink nipples against the flimsy fabric of her nightgown. The damp cling of her panties. The soft pout of her lips just begging to be kissed.

"I'm sure a million girls would sign up right now to be your phantom lover," Alana titters. Fergus glares at her. "Tell us more about what you fantasize about. Give us something to sink our teeth into. What's your ideal woman like? Can you describe her?"

As a matter of fact, I can. *But if I describe her to you now in all her wet dream-like glory, we're going to have a very awkward situation on our hands.*

I've given them a half an hour of my time and that's all they're getting. Something much more important requires my undivided attention.

My Tennessee angel.

I stand up, hoping like hell no one notices that I'm half-cocked already. "This interview is over. I've got somewhere I need to be."

They all stare at me as I walk out.

6

Outside, the sky is azure. It's eight fifteen and already ninety-two degrees.

Momma's cooking omelets and Gigi's doing some last-minute studying before a test. Rose is up, which is unusual. When she's in a funk, which is most of the time, she stays in bed half the day when she's not working. But she has a date tonight. Which means she'll spend all day preparing for it. I think it's sort of ridiculous that her mood swings are all about her boyfriend's whims. I've already decided I'm never going to let a man decide whether I'm happy or not, although when I said that to Rose she laughed and told me I have no idea about anything.

"I got a job," I tell them, before Momma can start grilling me.

They all look up.

"Where?" asks Momma.

"I met the new owner of the house next door yesterday."

Gigi looks up from her book. "What new owner?" I was worried she overheard some of our conversation last night, but when I crept back into the window and quietly closed the screen I could tell by her breathing she was still fast asleep.

"He said his name is Travis. He bought the house and he's looking for a cleaner."

"Who is he?" Momma's hand is on her hip, like he's a criminal or something and she already doesn't trust him.

I grab a piece of toast from a plate on the table. "I don't know his life story. All I know is that he bought the house. He said he won't be home all that much but he wants someone to do some dusting and weed the garden. He seems nice." Mostly all true.

"I don't know if that's a good idea," Momma says. "I'll need to meet him first."

"I told you, he's not home. And he wanted me to start this morning. He had to head back to work, he said, early this morning. It's perfect, really. It's close by and he said I can practice on his piano anytime I want."

Momma's eyeing me like now it's me she doesn't trust. She doesn't like that my dream is to become a musician, so I don't talk about it much. She thinks it's frivolous and unrealistic. She wants me to go to college and become a teacher. Which isn't something I'd ever do. The thing is, I inherited my mother's grit and she knows this. She can see it reflecting right back at her whenever she looks at me, she said that to me once. Besides, she knows better than anyone that a job is a job.

I breeze past her reservations. "I'll mention that you'd like to meet him, if you insist, but you'll have to wait until he gets home."

"What does he do?" asks Gigi.

"He didn't say."

Gi closes her book. "I've always wondered what that house looks like inside."

"I can give you a tour." It's strange, though. I already feel a thread of possessiveness for Travis and whatever time I might get to spend with him. And if we go swimming ... "But let's wait until another day, when I know he'll be there, so I can introduce you. I'm not sure about his schedule."

"Did he discuss how much he's going to pay you?" Momma asks.

I don't know why I lie, and I'm not proud of it. "I think he said minimum wage. I'll double check." I just don't know how that would sound, if I were to tell it like it is. She'll wonder why he would pay so much. In fact I'm wondering the same thing myself. *Well, Momma, he's going to pay me a hundred dollars an hour to dust his piano. And then we're going to go for a swim together in his pond because it sounds like fun. Dangerously tempting fun, maybe, especially since I'll be wearing Scarlett's skimpiest bikini because the only bathing suit I own looks like it should have died last century and it also got taken out with the trash this morning.*

I don't have to feel guilty about it, I remind myself. A little white lie or a small omission will spare Momma from worrying about me. It's the kind thing to do, especially since I've already made up my mind. I've done my time and followed all the rules. I'm free now to walk my own path and make my own decisions. If I want to go for a swim with Travis, then I will.

I stand up and grab my bag.

"What about breakfast?" Momma says.

"I had a piece of toast." I grab a banana. "I'll see you later. Good luck on your test, Gi."

Momma's still eyeing me but I kiss her on the cheek.

"It's all good," I assure her. "I'm dusting some furniture and mopping a few floors in an empty house. I'll see you at dinnertime."

She relents and goes back to her cooking.

I feel a weight lift as soon as I climb the fence. The day is the most beautiful day I can remember. Maybe because my future shines so bright.

I think about taking a swim before I go inside Travis's house but I want to get started.

Dusting his piano.

For *a hundred* dollars an hour.

It's ridiculous, but I've already decided I'm going to earn my money fair and square. I'm going to clean his house so well he won't even recognize it. I'll restore it to its former glory.

Travis has left the window wide open for me. I step through it.

There's a note on the piano, held down with a bottle of whiskey that's about two-thirds full.

> Ruby,
> Don't worry about anything except the music.
> Write a new song. Practice the ones you've got. And be ready for that swim when I get back.
> T

I decide to give myself a tour of the house. I've never looked around before because I didn't want to trespass any more than I already was.

I think about what might happen later. I remember what he said, about the swim. The way his eyes got all dark and intense. Just before he *almost* kissed me. *You know you want to, darlin'.* Just thinking about it brings a flush to my skin. The one I'm starting to get used to, whenever I think about Travis.

I'm wearing jean shorts and a pink tank top over Scarlett's white bikini. Who knows, we might not even have time for swimming. Or he might have changed his mind.

The house is beautiful. Dusty but majestic. It's about twice the size of our own house, and much fancier. Hazy sunlight filters in through bay windows that look out toward the pond and over the view of the hills. The wood floors are smooth and there's a large stone fireplace. Up the curved staircase, there are four large bedrooms and three bathrooms. And up another flight of stairs, there's a master bedroom with its own enormous master bathroom and even its own little balcony.

It's dusty, like the rest of the house.

It doesn't look like he slept up here.

I go to the French doors leading out onto the balcony and open them, stepping out.

Wow.

He's got an amazing view. I can see the edge of the pond but not my house, which is obscured by the high roof. The view is westward, toward Nashville. "Here I come," I whisper, without meaning to. It sounds foolish but I don't care. I actually twirl around in the dazzling sun because I'm so *happy*. Now I'll be able to save enough to rent a room and to buy a phone that's good enough to record my songs on. Maybe I'll even upload them straight onto one of those music apps Rose was telling me about. Those ones you can earn money on if people listen to your songs. Maybe I'll get discovered and my hits will go viral, whatever that is. Maybe

I really *will* be able to sing for a living. And travel all over the country on tour and see the whole world. I can taste the promise of my own success like sugar on my tongue.

I go back inside, into the master bathroom. Under the sink I find some cleaning supplies. I decide to start in this room. I'll clean up his bedroom so he can sleep here tonight. I don't want him changing his mind about hiring me.

The house has everything. A linen closet full of sheets. Towels. A washing machine and a dryer. So I clean the bedding and make his bed. I disinfect the bathroom and vacuum the hardwood floors.

I stand back to admire my work. The place looks good. More than good. It's the nicest bedroom I've ever seen.

Then I go downstairs to the piano.

I read his note again, picking up the whiskey bottle. It occurs to me that *he* would have drunk out of it. I don't see a glass anywhere. Slowly, I unscrew the lid. *His mouth might have touched it.*

I touch my tongue to the rim. And I take a sip. Just to see what it tastes like. It burns all the way down and makes me cough. But the burn turns warm and mellow. I take another sip.

Then I put the lid back on and set it on the piano.

I dust the surface of it until the wood gleams. But I'm too hyped up to sit and play. It's so hot. I go into the kitchen, which is huge with granite counters, fancy new appliances and another set of French doors that lead out to a cute outdoor dining area. I open the French doors to let in the light breeze. And I let myself fantasize about what it would be like to live in a house like this.

The kitchen is just as dusty as the rest of the house. I might as well do some cleaning in here, too, in case he wants to cook something. So I pour some soap into a bucket and fill it with hot water. I can't find a mop but there's a large sponge so I throw that into the bucket too.

A radio is sitting on the counter. I turn it on and crank it up.

And what do you know, the song comes on. *That* song. The one about the wild, wild girl and the hot summer night.

It's obviously a hit if it's being played so much. You can see why. It's catchy and soulful, touching that rare sweet spot between originality, talent and commercial perfection. And that *voice*. That husked croon that hits me right where I live. I'm on my hands and knees, scrubbing the floor with the soapy sponge. Strands of my hair have come loose from my ponytail. And damn this bikini. I'm practically falling out of my tank top. My short shorts feel too tight. The bikini bottom has bunched up and is rubbing against me in a way that feels sort of … *good*. I'm sweating and getting all worked up over this damn song again. I don't just feel hot, I feel *hot*. Like all my new urges are on overdrive.

And as I listen more closely to the song, I realize it: the voice sounds *familiar*. That dark, sexy rasp.

But no. It couldn't be. It's a big wide world out there. Just because one guy sang me a song doesn't mean he's the only one in the world who's got a deep, husky voice.

As I work and the beginnings of a sensuous rise tease me, I hum along to the tune.

I'm not the only one.

That's when I realize Travis is *standing* there, singing softly along with me, watching me. I didn't hear him come in. He's leaning against the door frame with his arms folded across his chest, all six-foot-something of sweaty, sun-burnished muscle, inked with a few artful designs, smoldering emerald-bright eyes and messily-smoothed hair. His masculinity sort of gleams and oozes, enveloping me in its invisible haze. He's wearing a pair of shorts.

And nothing else.

God. He's so big and muscular.

I freeze but I can feel my heartbeat, not just in my chest. *Between my legs.* I can feel his presence *right there.* Where I'm warm and wet. Where the sweetness aches.

"Hey, Ruby."

I stand up and smooth my clothes self-consciously, realizing how I must look. "Hey, Travis."

"What are you doing?"

"Cleaning your house, like I said I would."

"You're supposed to be working on your music."

"I will. I just … I had some energy to burn."

"Is that right?" he says softly.

"Yeah."

God.

I feel like I'm about to melt into a puddle right here in front of him. My whole body feels supple and hot, simmering with that honeyed heat. I notice it then: a huge, bulky, swollen ridge inside his shorts.

Oh.

My heart's racing. I lean against the coolness of the marble counter, holding onto it for support.

"I don't want you cleaning anymore, all right?" He walks past me, close to me, as he goes to the fridge and opens it. "You want a drink?"

"Sure."

He grabs two bottles of Budweiser, opens them and hands me one. I take it.

I've never drunk beer before but I don't tell him this. *New life, new rules.* I take a sip. It's bitter and cold. I'm so thirsty I drink about a third of it in one long sip. Then I drink a little more. Travis smiles.

"Did you play the piano?" he asks me.

"Not yet. I was just about to."

"So, let me get this straight. The one thing I asked you to do … you didn't even do." He seems more amused by this than riled.

"I dusted it."

"I want you to play it. That's our deal. You play your songs and write more."

God, he's bossy. "I *will*. I promise."

"We've got time. We've got all summer, right?"

"Yeah." The day's hot and the beer's cold so I drink some more. It tastes good and the world's taken on a sparkly edge. We're watching each other's eyes.

A current of heat seems to fizzle in the air between us. No doubt about it: hell, here I come.

He smiles again, as though he's reading my mind. "Come on." He flicks his head sideways as a light command to follow him. "Let's go for that swim."

"It's a scorcher," he says, as we walk toward the pond.

"Yeah, it's hot."

This is it. We're really going swimming together.

"Where did you move from?" I don't know a thing about him. And I'm sort of craving more information beyond the fact that he possesses the ability to practically set me on fire with one flick of his green glance. I'm riveted by the way his thick hair falls across his forehead. The graceful, gilded shape of his broad shoulders and the color of his skin. "Where did you live before you moved here?"

"I've got a couple of houses."

"Oh." He seems almost cagey about telling me too

much. "What made you want to move all the way out here?"

He grins down at me from his six feet something of muscled, hair-dusted brawn. "I wanted some privacy. I needed a place to get away from it all. Where nobody knows me and where I can hear myself think."

"You can't think at your other houses?"

His smile lingers. "No. Not really."

I wait for him to elaborate but he doesn't. "What kind of work do you do?"

We're at the water's edge. There are layers to both his silence and his amusement I don't fully understand. I don't want to pry but I'm wondering where he got all his money.

Travis walks straight into the pond and dives under. He swims out and flicks the water from his hair in that way hot guys do. He waits for me.

I don't immediately strip down to my bikini. I'm wishing it wasn't quite as non-existent as it is. I mean, sure, he's seen me already but I wasn't *aware* of that at the time until after the fact.

I wade in to my ankles and splash the water lightly with my feet.

He crooks a finger at me, signaling for me to come in.

Maybe it's the whiskey or the beer talking but to hell with it. I can't swim with my shorts on anyway. So I unbutton them and slide them down my legs, stepping out of them. I peel off my tank top, tossing it aside, and pull out my hair-tie, letting my hair spill over my shoulders. It hangs all the way down my back in loose coils.

As he watches me, Travis's jaw literally drops.

It's the first time in my life I've felt a feminine kind of … *power* that's new to me. I don't know why but I *like* that he's riveted and speechless. There's something empowering about holding this big, brawny *male* in my invisible grasp just with the flick of a curl and the feminine shape of my body. I want to … connect. And explore. I know he can enlighten me about things I've wondered about. I know he *is* going to enlighten me. I'm ready. In my mind and my body, I'm choosing him. I'm choosing to be as adventurous as I dare.

I make a half-hearted attempt to adjust my bikini into place but it's a lost cause. There's nothing to adjust. The little triangles of the top cover my nipples but not much else. My breasts are way too full for it. I can feel his gaze like the hot sun on my skin.

I shouldn't be doing any of this, of course. Like I shouldn't listen to rock 'n roll or pursue my passion even though I'm good at it because it's not the proper, straight and narrow thing to do. Sister Louise would have a conniption if she could see me right now.

Good thing she can't.

I always knew I wasn't straight and narrow. *Or* proper. They tried to train my gentle rebellion out of me. Maybe they partly did, for a while. But not anymore. A fire's been lit under my rebellion. It's a fire called life itself. I refuse to back away from it any longer.

I'm already damned, maybe, and so be it. Might as well savor the hell out of my fall. Travis and I are under each other's spell, just me and him here alone under the sun, writing our own song.

He swims toward me. He walks out of the water and towers over me, standing close enough for the tiny stinging droplets to drip onto my skin. I laugh and try to move away but he grabs my wrist in his strong grip. "Don't run."

He's touching me.

"You're so fucking beautiful." His voice is low with a hushed awe.

I'm a little taken aback by it. Not just by the crass suddenness of the delivery, but that … *he thinks I'm beautiful.* I could sort of tell by the way he's looking at me, but still. I don't get a lot of compliments from the nuns. Or my sisters, aside from Gi. I also don't hear a lot of swearing. But I like the way it sounds when Travis does it. Sort of … *aggressive.*

He smiles, noticing the mild shock on my face. "Let me hear you say it," he says.

"Say what?"

"A swear word. Have you ever said one?"

"Sure. I say them all the time," I laugh, but it's a lie and he knows it. The nuns make you pray for forgiveness.

"Let me hear it."

"No." I can feel myself blush. Is it *that* obvious? That I'm a prim, inexperienced hick?

"You're wilder than you let on," he says.

He's right. I feel bold and luck-drunk. And maybe even *drunk*-drunk.

You're my wild, wild girl and I know what you like. Let's go for a ride on a hot summer night.

At his touch, my inhibitions fade back, like mist on an August morning. I let him pull me into deeper water. I let go of his hand to swim, keeping a safe distance. He circles me like a shark and I can feel the current of his movement swirling around me, caressing me in sultry ripples. His smile is playful and gorgeous.

We reach the low edge of the flat rock. I climb up onto it and he follows.

Knowing he's coming after me ... so close to me ... it starts the warm, humming heat, which builds and centers. I feel the slickness gather, the light, aching throb. He's right behind me. The huge, hot bulk of him is almost touching me.

God.

It's so clear now why they kept the boys away from us, when their effect is *this* potent. He's like a living magnet, melting away all my defenses and hesitations, stoking all my animal urges until I can feel them pulsing intimately.

I crawl further onto the rock and lay on its smooth, sun-warmed surface. Travis lays next to me, propping his head on his bent arm.

His eyes are light in the sun. "I thought about you all morning," he says. "And all night."

"You did?"

"Yeah. I did."

"I thought about you too."

"Yeah?"

"I almost woke up my sister last night because I was humming along to the song we sang together."

"It's a good song."

"Thanks."

His eyelashes are tipped with tiny jewel-drops. "How old are you?" he asks me.

"Eighteen."

Travis smiles. "Good."

"How old are you?"

"I just turned twenty-five last week."

Wow. He's a lot older than me. Clearly much more worldly. More experienced. More *everything*. And I wonder if I'm getting in over my head just being here with him like this. "Happy birthday."

He lays back, all hard contours and rippling muscles, glistening and wet. "Thanks."

"Did you do anything special?" I regret the question as soon as I've asked it. It sounds like small town chitchat.

"Yeah. I did."

I can't tell if he's deliberately withholding information —or why he would—or if he's teasing me, playing with my curiosity. Luckily I'm just as stubborn as he is. "What did you do?"

Travis smiles. "Had a party."

"That's cool."

He laughs. "Sure."

He can tease me and I can tease him right back. "With who?"

"My brothers. And my sister. And a few other people." He changes the subject, back to me. "You've got two sisters?"

"Three. One's married and lives in Knoxville. I've only been there once. Believe it or not, I've never even been out of the state of Tennessee. Actually that's not true. Gigi and I once drove over the state line of Kentucky after she got her license just to see what it would feel like."

"How did it feel?"

"Not much different than it does here."

It's not fair that he's able to pry information out of me but is unwilling to give me much in return. I'm about to ask him more about his family but he coils a finger around an end lock of my wet hair. "You're seriously blowing my mind right now," he murmurs. "I just can't get over you, darlin'. I keep thinking I'm dreaming."

He's sweet and he's … beautiful. I want to do it so badly. So I do. I reach out to touch his dripping hair, gently fingering the wet locks, like he's doing to mine. His hair is as thick as it looks.

Travis leans closer and kisses my lips. It's sudden, without a hint of hesitation. I've never kissed anyone before. I mean, Chase, but that was a long time ago and it was hardly even a kiss. I'm not sure how to even do it. I let my lips press against his. But Travis's mouth is *hungry*. I gasp as he boldly parts my lips with his tongue, caressing my lips with his, opening me. I'm not surprised that he has all the confidence of an ultra-virile alpha in the prime of his life but I'm not entirely prepared for it. There's nothing tentative about him and I don't know what I was expecting but not quite ... *this.*

His tongue slides over mine and I can feel the contact as a zinging surge that stokes the sweet ache. Reflexively, my knees separate a little. He moves, crouching over me like a big cat. He lowers his body over mine, holding himself above me, and I tense.

The hardness of him.

The weight of his muscular body is stunning. He lays himself over me more heavily, pressing me *there*, with *himself.*

Oh my God.

My heart is thumping and I'm breathing hard.

It's so fast and so ... *rough.* He's big and playful and cocky as hell.

Travis gazes down at me with that lazy smile. He likes my shyness. He's playing with it, challenging me to resist him. *Daring* me with his eyes.

"Don't be scared of me," he says. "We'll go as slow as you want."

"I'm not scared." Even though I am, just a little. Scared and galvanized and alive and so turned on I feel dizzy. This is what I want and need: all these zinging surges of emotion and sensation that make my heart beat faster.

He goes still for a few seconds, allowing me to adjust to … *what he's doing.* Holding his weight to pin me in place, skin to skin. Not enough to hurt me or scare me. But it's a fine line.

Softly, he starts singing. My song.

Give me everything. I'm on my way. My dreams whispered promises that won't fade away. I want to burn and I want to fly. I don't have it in me not to live and to try.

I wrote those words. He's reminding me of that. And he's right.

"You want to burn and fly right now, darlin'?" The edgy heat in his smoky voice has a physical effect on me. It only compounds the warm, melting effect of his hard body.

I don't know what he means. All right, I *do* know what he means. The low, wild thrill of his hardness pressing against me is *already* making me fly a little, if you really want to know.

"Do you want another kiss, Ruby Hayes?"

His half-grin makes any doubt or resistance downright

laughable. He's too gorgeous to resist. I gaze up into those green eyes and I hear myself whisper, "Yes."

It's all the invitation he needs. His mouth takes mine, more gently this time but still with that brimming, voracious hunger.

This time when he dips his tongue into my mouth, I gently suck him deeper.

Travis groans, angling my head, invading me in soft, greedy plunges. His tongue dances with mine and he adjusts his heavy body against me, until I can feel the hard contours of his huge bulk between my legs, where the softness of my body molds around his hard shape, cradling him. Travis presses against the most sensitive place imaginable.

Oh.

He moves again … until I know what might happen. That *thing* that happened yesterday, when I touched myself. Except this bliss promises to be a hundred times more powerful.

"Travis," I gasp, overwhelmed.

"We'll take it nice and slow, baby." But even as he's saying it, he's holding me down so I can't move, pressing against me again. I moan lightly.

I don't even mean to do it but my hips arch against him a little, as though trying to find more of that building sensation.

"Hold still, sweetheart. I know you're getting close. I can feel you. But I want to taste you when you come."

What?

Oh my God.

He kisses me again, longer this time, until every taste, every stroke of his tongue sends a fresh wave of warmth to my core. He nips at my lips then his mouth moves to my neck, licking the delicate skin below my ear. Every nip of his teeth on my skin sends a dart of pleasure to the hot hollow between my legs, which feels slippery and needy, making me squirm. A hot-sweet glow has ignited me from my knees to my navel.

Our breathing is heavier now. I let my hands glide to his neck, his hard shoulders. The textures and shape and size of him are dizzying … he's so deliciously *powerful.*

His mouth kisses little nips down my breast. His lips touch my nipple through the thin fabric of my bikini. His teeth, in a gentle demand, bite me.

The throb swells, and I gasp. I think it might happen. It *is* happening. *Almost.* I'm so wet. I'm so desperate for more. And he's kissing me again. "You want me to kiss you, darlin'?" he murmurs against me. "You want me to eat you and suck on you and make you come?"

God help me. *Yes.*

The urges of my body are wild and hot, insanely extreme. If the nuns could see me now they'd lock me up for good and throw away the key.

Travis rips my bikini loose until the tiny triangles fall away, revealing the fullness of my naked breasts.

He's kissing my skin, whispering lust-slurred, wicked

words. Words I've barely even heard and never in a million years *used*.

Fuck, you're gorgeous. Should I see if I can make you come just like this? 'Cause I think you're just about there already. Let's see what happens when I do this. What do you say, darlin'?

I moan as his fingers gently pinch my nipple.

"You want me to suck on you real sweet, baby? Or hard and rough? Let's find out what you like."

Of course it occurs to me that we're going way too fast. That I'm jumping in to the ridiculously deep end without even knowing how to swim. But it's too late to protest or pull away. I'm already riding the crest of a pleasure wave that's going to be the most intense thing that's ever happened to me.

"Say it," he murmurs, swirling his tongue around my nipple.

"*Please, Travis.*"

"Good girl. Easy now."

If he doesn't do it right now I'm going to wrap myself around him and keep him there until he does. I'm going to beg and plead for that mouth to kiss me and that tongue to lick me. The needy ache is a roaring wildfire in me.

And then he does it. His mouth closes around my nipple and he begins to suck me into his hot mouth. His tongue licks the underside of my nipple in rough laves, then he draws more deeply, sucking in greedy pulls. He pinches my other nipple between two fingers, rotating gently. His palm cups my breast, squeezing and pinching. It's warm, so warm, feeding the heat of my body. I melt, just like that, the sweet rushes surging lushly through my body.

Travis laughs softly. "Damn, you're a hot little thing."

I'm still riding the ripples when I feel the callouses of his rough hands wander over the soft skin of my thighs. His fingers ... *oh, God* ... they're sliding closer ... closer. Until he's rubbing his fingers over the fabric of my bikini. *There. Pushing the cloth aside—oh, hell*—until his fingers slide over my sensitive, swollen flesh, finding the little hyper-sensitive nub where his fingertips glide with deliberate pressure as his mouth feasts on my nipples in lusty pulls.

It happens again.

The pleasure compounds into a million stars of clenching ecstasy. I'm flying. I'm in love with life. I'm in love with him and his mouth and his fingers.

I float. Until the waves slowly begin to calm.

There's a tiny voice at the back of my mind. *You've gone too far and too fast. You're naked and coming hard and sinning like it's going out of style. Go home right now. Be good like you know you should.*

But I can't move. I don't want to move.

This feels far too good to stop now.

We're so ravenous it hurts.

My hands are gripping his brawny arms. His mouth leaves my breast and he's sliding lower, licking his way down my stomach. He yanks the ties at the side of my bikini bottom and it falls completely off.

"Hold still, sweetheart. I'm going to kiss you real good." His *voice*. With its edge of darkness and roughed-up desire. I think he could make me come by just murmuring his sweet, dirty words. "Right where you want me to. Nice and slow."

Oh, God. He's going to do that thing that Rose was talking about.

He pushes my legs wider with brutal strength, holding me down, dominating me easily. My intimate muscles are still fluttering. His mouth is so close I can feel the hot strikes of his breath.

Well, this is a whole new kind of education. Because, just then, his tongue licks into me. This is not a soft, hesitant initiation. This is lewd, insatiable worship. It's wet, hungry, debauched. His tongue is everywhere, tasting and feasting with messy adoration. His rough, careful fingers are ridiculously intimate, sliding through the moisture, prodding and pressing gently. Opening me. Touching me in places I've never been touched. His mouth closes around the pulsing nub and the rushes are starting again. His hold gentles and his tongue dips into me, pushing deeper, in and out. His thumb finds my nub, swirling it, pressing. I come again, hard. His tongue is inside me and I can feel my inner muscles gently squeezing as he tastes me.

The starry rush goes on and on.

As the waves begin to ease, he keeps on licking and

kissing me, playing me with his fingers. The intimacy is astounding.

After a while, he crawls up my body and lays next to me. He's smiling and it's the most sublime sight, his eyes all sparkly and green.

He's staring deep into my eyes and the link is profound and connective. "You taste like heaven when you come. Just like I knew you would."

How do I reply to such a thing?

I touch my hand to his chest and I notice then that his —*wow*. His … *manhood* is halfway out of his unbuttoned shorts. I'm very shocked by the sight of it. I mean, I'm not *that* naïve. I have three older sisters, after all. Two of them are … experienced, and they've told me things. A lot of things. But this … it's not at all what I was expecting. It's big. *Huge*. Much bigger than I would have thought. And dizzyingly *hard*. It's rounded at the head and … *wet*. Sort of dusky and hot-looking and shiny with moisture.

He laughs at my expression. "That must have been a very strict boarding school."

I'm still mesmerized by what I'm seeing. "It was."

"Don't be scared of me, baby. Go ahead and touch if you want."

Maybe it's the beer I chugged, or the enlightenment of back-to-back orgasms—or both—because I *do* want to. I want to touch him.

Once you get a taste for the devil, there's no turning back, as it turns out.

Travis kisses me and it's the most outrageous thing, to taste *myself* on his lips. He lays back, pulling me along with him so I'm half on top of him.

My naked body still hums with the after-effects of my rushes. Tentatively, I smooth my fingers across the feather inked to his muscular shoulder. Along his hair-dusted chest. And lower. I run my fingers over the tight grooves of his six pack. He has a tattoo low across his stomach, a decorative line of musical notes. Everything about him fascinates me. "What's the song?" I whisper, as my fingers rove.

"The first song I ever wrote."

He gives me time to explore him, to run my fingers over the textures of his body. I've never touched a man, and certainly not like this. He's a work of art, is the damn truth. All sculpted and bronzed. I let my fingers rove the darker arrow line of hair on his lower stomach.

I'm getting closer.

To *it*.

To his gigantic *cock*, Rose and Scarlett call it.

If my sisters are brave enough to do this, then so am I. Slowly, I let my hand ease around the thick length, rubbing my palm across the silky bulk. Another small gush of liquid seeps out the end.

Travis groans.

A primal wash of longing floods through me.

"Can I kiss you?" I whisper, shocked by my words but also not. Scarlett did this, she told me. *Men will kill for you if you do that to them*, she said, which at the time I thought was a crazy thing to say. *They'll fall in love with you, that's how much they love it.*

His eyes are hot and lust-drowsed. "You can do any damn thing you want, sweetheart."

I slide both my palms gently along his slick, solid length. I finger the ridge of the crown and the small slit. I swirl the bead of moisture that's leaking there, and touch my finger to my tongue.

Travis is watching me. "Jesus, baby. You get me so damn hot."

I can see that what I'm doing to him is almost painfully pleasurable for him. I squeeze him gently, tightening my grip.

I hardly recognize myself. I'm *thirsty*. For him.

So I do it. I lean forward and touch my tongue to the slippery tip of his cock, licking him lightly.

His head falls back and he growls some filthy words. So I lick him again. I put my lips around the broad end and take him deeper, sucking on him carefully.

"Ruby," he's moaning. "Ruby." Over and over. He's praying.

I suck harder.

And then it happens. His cock starts to jerk. Scarlett described this part. It shocked the hell out of me when she first told me but now I'm glad she did. So I'm at least partly prepared when milky liquid jets into my mouth in hot bursts. I drink some but there's too much. It spills down my chin and my hands, dripping onto my breasts.

It's the most beautiful thing in the world. Me, naked, covered in his seed, drinking it, holding him as it pulses out of him. A sticky bond. An intimacy from which we'll never recover.

He pulls me up to him and I'm lying on top of him. He wipes my mouth gently with his thumb. His eyes are lust-drowsed and awestruck. "My Tennessee angel," he whispers.

"You taste like heaven when you come," I whisper. It's true. He's the most religious thing that's ever happened to me.

7

———

TRAVIS

HOLY FUCK.

She's covered in my cum. It's dripping down her chin and onto those unbelievably perfect breasts. Her lips are pink and wet. She's lying on top of me and I want everything about this girl so badly already I'll chase after her if she walks away from me. That's all there is to it and I don't even want to think about how far it goes or what this even means.

It's a brutal, dug-in kind of a lust, like a madness.

I've never experienced anything like Ruby Hayes in my goddamn life. And I'm pretty sure … she doesn't even know who I am.

I'm already hard again. All I can do is sort of gaze up at her like an idiot. She's got this insane, copper-tinted blond hair that's soft as silk, like a mermaid's might be. She's got that aura, of otherworldliness.

There's not a goddamn thing that's even remotely ordinary about her.

The curves of her body are lusciously youthful and feminine. She's a unicorn of an experience. Once you see her and *feel* her and get close to her, you'll never recover.

What makes it even worse is that she's as pure as the goddamn driven snow. I can tell by the way she moves. She comes across as both innocent and horny as fuck.

I'm so fucked.

Words don't even.

When she stripped down to her bikini I almost started coming just *looking* at her. Riding a weird sure thing, where you can barely hold on to it and you're existing in this state of pure, white-hot anticipation.

She tastes like a sweet, warm, exotic fruit.

She's lying on top of me. I just came in her mouth but my cock has realized its purpose and here it is. Downtime is not an option, apparently.

I know she's a virgin. She's innocent and naïve but her inexperience is overridden almost completely by a lust-edge sense of adventure. My girl's got a twinkle in her eye. She was always going to get her halo dirty, first chance she got. It's as though she just discovered the beauty of her own body and *loves* it.

I love it too.

I love it.

I don't want her to climb off of me. I'm holding her round, firm ass in my hands as she kisses me. My fingers play, touching her warm, slick folds. She's not shaved or waxed or whatever but has a fine, blond fur that's without a doubt the sexiest damn thing I've ever seen and makes me feel like I've morphed into a fucking caveman. She's writhing softly on top of me and the lips of her pussy press against the base of my cock. *I'm so close.* I could so easily position her, slide my hot cock right on into that juicy nirvana.

She'd let me. She wouldn't stop me. I know this, but I don't do it. Not yet. It's not just that I don't have a condom with me. There's more to it than that. I don't want to fuck this up. I don't want to rush it and scare her off by doing anything she might regret.

Not that she seems like she's regretting much of anything right about now. That squirming little body is burning up. She's doing this soft, rhythmic grind against my cock. She's breathing in quiet huffs. She might be about to come. Again.

She *is* about to come.

She's looking into my eyes now. Those clear, amber-gold eyes have this tender, transfixed glow, like she loves me or something. I know that look. What's different about this look is that I *feel* it. I *want* her to look at me like that. I want to drink in her adoration, and earn more of it. Her sun-pink hair frames her face. Silken ropes of it feather along my skin.

I'm so fucked.

"Travis," she whispers.

So I give her what she wants. I'm almost surprised by what comes out of my mouth. "That's it, darlin'. I'm going to hold onto you and make you come again, just like you like it, sweet baby. You're so sweet. I'll take such good care of you. Kiss me, Ruby. Give me your mouth."

She does but she's speechless by now. I glide my fingers across her clit, and I gently press into her pussy and her ass. She's so tight but so damn wet. I go deeper than I did before. I pull her closer, rubbing her clit with my cock, gliding against the little nub as I suck on her tongue.

She's coming.

She's whimpering into my mouth. Her body's writhing softly against me.

I can feel the luscious tightening of her pussy pulsing around my fingers … and against my cock, which is pressed against her.

Oh, fuck. *I'm* coming.

I'm coming.

Holy hell, she feels so damn good. Hot surges of my cum wet her stomach, and mine, creating a slick stickiness between us, like glue. I wish it *was* glue. I wish I could keep her here, all to myself. I want to fuck her and kiss her whenever I want.

My hands are on her ass. Her hips. I cradle her head against my neck. My fingers trace along the lines of her body. I carefully brush a strand of her hair back from her face.

And I just hold her like that for a while.

It feels so good, just us, here, in the sun. Tripping on our own kind of drug. Riding the high of our own rush and letting it calm, her body fitting perfectly against mine.

After a while, I murmur. "Ruby? You okay?"

"Yeah," she breathes quietly. "Don't move yet. I just want to stay here."

After a minute, she lifts her head, looking at me. She's sort of drowsed-looking, drunk with the after-effects of her pleasure.

I've never seen eyes the color of hers. Amber, with bright flecks of gold.

She's so damn *beautiful*.

She kisses my lips softly. "Travis," she murmurs. "What's your last name?"

"Tucker. Travis Tucker." I almost panic. She doesn't know who I am and I don't want her to. I want her to want me for this. For *me*. Without all the hype.

I wait for the familiarity to click as I watch her eyes but it doesn't. She really doesn't know who I am.

I'm about to suggest we go back to the house and eat something. I know if I kiss her back, if I surrender to the soft touch of her tongue, if I let this go in the direction it inevitably will, we'll end up taking it further. My cock will be inside her very soon if we don't get up and move …

and I can't believe I'm saying this, but it's not the right time.

I can't believe I'm saying this either, but I want it to be perfect.

Just then I hear the unmistakable sound of the deep, loud bass beats of a car stereo.

What the fuck.

The sound is coming from my own driveway. But how?

Then I remember: I described the route. The one and only person I told about the location of my new property.

Vaughn.

Ruby hears it too. "You have visitors. Who is it?"

"My brother."

The driveway is on the far side of the house, but she eases herself off me. I feel unreasonably upset by this. I don't want her to get dressed. I don't want her to leave me. I want to keep her here, naked, with me, alone.

Get a goddamn grip, Travis.

I help her, pulling up my shorts as I stand up. I grab her shorts from where she'd stepped out of them. She's standing there, covered in my cum, practically from head to toe. I experience a rush of caveman-like satisfaction at this that's so wildly overblown I hardly recognize myself. *She's mine. I've marked her as my own by coming all over her naked body.* Just seeing her like this makes me go instantly hard again.

"I guess I better wash off a little," she smiles at me, weaving her fingers through mine.

I hear voices in the distance. Vaughn's not alone. *I'll kill him.* I gave him strict instructions not to tell anyone where this place is.

Didn't I?

The very last thing I need is another swarm of groupies or the goddamn paparazzi setting up camp outside my new house. It took them all of one day to figure out where our headquarters in Nashville were located after we bought it. Our fans swarmed the entrance and they've basically been there ever since. It's annoying as fuck.

The other thing that's annoying as fuck is this: if I take Ruby back to the house with me, Vaughn—and whoever's with him—will see her. They'll see her strawberry-blond hair and her golden eyes. They'll watch her, in her little jean shorts and her tank top—which she'll have to wear with nothing under it since her bikini is wet. They'll see her perfect breasts and the way her nipples poke up against the fabric.

No fucking way.

She's mine.

She's standing knee-deep in the water, splashing handfuls across her breasts and stomach. She's leaning forward and I can see her pussy—still wet and flushed from my greedy mouth. *I want to eat her again. I want to take her to bed and never let her go.* I pull my shorts up, shoving my rampant hard-on in, somehow, willing it to go down.

Goddamn it. There's no way in hell. Not with the sight of her as she's splashing herself. She leans forward to pick up her shirt.

I'm going crazy.

I'm almost relieved when she says, "I better get going. It's getting late. Even though it would be fun to meet your brother."

"He's … " *Insane. Completely unscrupulous. Entirely untrustworthy around a goddess like you.* " … you can meet him another time."

We're dressed now but I feel pissed off and out of my mind. I don't want her to go. The thought of waiting hours to see again her is almost unbearable. And I remember now that we have a show tomorrow night, in the city. I'd almost forgotten about it.

I'd forgotten everything except Ruby and her face and her hair and her sweet, ludicrously luscious body.

We have something booked for tomorrow morning, I remember. Then our show tomorrow night and an interview with Rolling Stone the morning after.

I kiss her lips and I really don't recognize myself. My eyes close as I taste her. And taste *us.* Our bond. Our lust. My own need, which feels bigger than the sun and the sky right about now. "Ruby," I hear myself saying, "I don't want to leave you. But I have work tomorrow. And tomorrow night. I won't be back until the next day. I'll come to you as soon as I can."

She kisses me back and—*oh, fuck*—my cock is so hard, so hot, and my mind is racing. I could take her away somewhere. I could get rid of Vaughn and skip the concert. I could disappear with my Tennessee angel and spend the rest of my life kissing her lips and licking her pussy, making sweet love to her until I die from the pleasure of her. *I can't take this.* "Oh." Like she's upset, too, that we won't be together again for two whole days. "That's okay. I can just let myself in. But I'll come back on Monday morning. If you want me to."

"Of course I do." I hear the urgency in my own voice. I feel weirdly, crazily desperate already, to get back to her. "I'll be back on Monday afternoon. Wait for me." Goddamn it, I sound like a love-struck fool. But I don't care. I want to hear her say it.

"Okay." She smiles and I can feel it in my chest. "I'll wait for you."

"And no more cleaning. Work on the songs. Write me a new one."

"All right, Travis." She smiles at me and it *hurts.* Everything about this is equal parts heaven and hell.

I kiss her. I touch my tongue to her soft lower lip. I open her lips with mine, dipping my tongue into her mouth, slayed by how good she tastes.

She pulls back, laughing lightly at my intensity. She

lets her hand slip from mine and I watch her wave as she walks away.

"See you on Monday," she chimes and I'm about to go after her but I force myself to stand there, to let her go. *You'll see her in two days, you lunatic.*

"You're beautiful," I call after her. "I'll miss you."

She blows me a kiss.

Holy hell, I am so fucked.

8

I TURN when I get around halfway to the fence and he's still watching me.

I laugh and wave to him once more and he makes a face, fighting against his own longing. He doesn't want me to go. *I'll miss you.*

Wow.

It's a crazy thing, lust. Attraction.

The feel of a man.

The taste of his cum as it floods in seedy bursts into your mouth.

I can still taste him. I can still feel his essence, inside me. Like drinking him has infused me with fire and heat and so much more. An awareness of myself and my own beauty.

And I've figured something out. Stellar orgasms change a person. Not only that, but stellar orgasms delivered by someone as beautiful and *hot* as Travis Tucker *transform* a person. It's true. I don't feel like a prim schoolgirl anymore. Not that I ever really did. But now, I'm sort of walking around in a haze of realization. And of simmering, hundred-proof summertime lust.

Travis Tucker.

I like his name. I always thought my name would look good in lights. His would too. I almost feel like I've heard that name somewhere before but I don't know where or why I would have.

And now that I know what Travis Tucker can *do*, with his hands and his mouth and his body, I'm wondering if I'll ever be able to get enough of it.

Part of me is addicted to Travis already. But a bigger part of me is addicted to *myself*. I love what he does to me. I love how he makes me feel. I want to immerse myself in all our entwining glory, to take everything he's willing to give. So I can experience to the deepest depths of what it means to be free and young and alive.

Dusk has begun to color the sky shades of purple and orange. It's later than I thought.

I enter the back door quietly and go into the bathroom. My mother would know something's happened to me, just by looking at me, I'm sure of it. And she hears me come in. "Is that you, Ruby?"

"Yeah, it's me, Momma. I'm dirty from working all day. I'm going to take a shower."

Shutting the door of the bathroom, I click the lock into place.

I turn on the water and let it run, and I stare at myself in the mirror. I look different. I look flushed and bright-eyed. My still-damp hair is loose and wild. My lips are puffy from his kisses. The skin of my jaw is pink from the roughness of his beard. *And so are my inner thighs.* I strip off my clothes.

I step into the shower and let the warm water wash over me. I run my fingers over my nipples ... *where he sucked on me until I came.*

If it's a sin, why does it feel so damn good?

I run my hands lightly over my stomach ... *where I'm still sticky from his cum.* I touch my fingers between my legs, remembering how it felt *when he licked me, tasting me as I came hard with his tongue inside me. How he rubbed his big, hard cock against me and made me come again.*

The pleasure waves would be easy to summon again, now, but I don't want to. I want *him* to do it.

I want him to do everything.

You just can't expect someone to get a taste of something like that and not want more of it. It would be like asking someone who's dying of thirst to take only a tiny sip of a tall, cool glass of water. I understand now what they were trying to protect us from. Ourselves and all our rich, crazy, beautiful desire.

I dry myself off and wrap the towel around me. Then I go into my room, dazed but at the same time lucid.

Tonight, I'm half wrecked and half enlightened. Colors look brighter. Music seems to filter right out of the air and into my head. I have so many ideas. Tunes, coming together, like I've just been plugged into some cosmic life force that's filtering its energy more brightly and more clearly than anything has ever been.

I no longer feel like I'm simmering with inspiration. Now, I'm *on fire* with it.

There's no sign of Gi and I remember she was filling in for someone today at work and she was going to go out with friends after.

Putting on a white cotton nightie, I slide up the screen and pick up my guitar. I go out to the bench where Travis and I sat together and I strum softly for a while.

I wonder what it would be like to play with *him*. To write with him. To sit at his piano together and sing the song he wrote about the Tennessee angel. Maybe one day soon I'll ask him if he wants to.

I sit there, immersed, letting the song take form.

The sun is out and I'm walking to his door. Will he kiss me, will he come back for more. Hot summer lovers and hot moonlit nights. The touch of his hand feels so true and so right. Tell me where will this road lead and how far does it wind. Take me all the way there, boy, and say you'll be mine. Tell me where does this road lead and where does it end. Oh, where does this road lead and where does it end.

I see headlights approaching. It's Gi. She drives into the driveway and parks next to the house. She walks over to sit with me. She's wearing her favorite light blue sundress and her hair catches light under the near-full moon. "How was work?" she asks me.

"It was good." Before I can say another word or even think about how much I'm going to confess, another car pulls into the end of the driveway and stops there.

Rose's boyfriend has a fancy red sports car. After a few minutes, she gets out. She shuts the passenger door and waits as he pulls away. She waves and watches the car drive off.

Then she sees us sitting under the oak tree. She comes over and sits between us. "I just had the best night of my entire life." I can tell by Rose's mussed-up hair and the flush on her cheeks that she's experiencing one of those very same euphoria rushes I had earlier. "I just had sex with Jack in the back seat of his car," she tells us, sort of dreamily. Sometimes I wonder what it would be like not to have sisters, who you tell everything to. My sisters are like living, connected extensions of my soul. "I cried, it felt so good."

"*Rose*," scolds Gi. "Please tell me you used protection this time." It's not actually fair to Gi that she has to be worrying about Rose taking precautions. She took me to the free clinic but I guess since Rose is older than Gi, she figures Rose can take care of herself.

Which Rose clearly isn't. "I meant to, I swear. But he didn't have anything. And I wasn't about to say no to him. He told me he *loved* me. How could I say no to that?"

Gi shakes her head. But Gi doesn't *know*. I happen to know she's only kissed one boy and that she's still in the dark about most things. Like I was. *Until Travis.*

"I wanted him to do everything he did," Rose insists. "Now I understand why they call it making love. It was so, so beautiful. I'm *so* in love with him." She has tears in her eyes.

Yesterday I might have been shocked. Today I understand how a girl can easily get carried away.

Rose holds both our hands. "I think he might ask me to marry him."

"Rose," says Gi. "Let's go to the clinic tomorrow and get you a morning after pill at least, though, okay? You need to be more careful."

"Gi, he *loves* me," Rose gushes.

"Let's get a ring on your finger before you hang all your hopes on that, Rosie," Gi says gently. Rose is a drama queen one day and a die-hard romantic the next. Gi, for all her romantic novels she reads and her soft, caring manner, is far more practical.

"Girls," Momma calls to us from inside the screen door. "Come in now. It's getting late."

As I lay in my bed, later, I can hear the low beat of music in the distance. His music. Like a pulse. Like a heartbeat. Like a deep, rhythmic promise.

Wait for me. I'll miss you.

I want to know what it feels like. To make love. To cry because it feels so good.

I don't, though, have any delusions about *falling* in love. And I have no intention at all of getting married. Not for a long time. If I do, it'll be years from now, after I get my career on track. After I've seen the world and played to a crowd of a thousand people. Not until I get my music heard.

What I want to do right now is to *feel*. To write about those feelings.

And then to leave. So I can follow my dreams and make them all come true.

Until then, I get this feeling it's going to be the hottest summer on record.

Tell me where does this road lead and where does it end.

9

TRAVIS

I GET BACK to the house and Vaughn's there along with fucking Jackson Cole. It's bad enough that Vaughn showed up. Bringing along our vapid opening act is more than I can handle right now. I'd never wanted Jackson to tour with us in the first place. He was a friend of Vaughn's whose first album broke out. His second record, which dropped just before the tour started, is nowhere near as good. Maybe his first one was a fluke, who knows. Either way, he's been irritating me from day one, with his loose way with women and his omnipresence. He thinks of himself as one of us. I don't.

"If you tell a single soul where this place is," I say to him, grabbing a fistful of his shirt because my nerves are shot at this point, "I'll kill you with my bare hands."

"Shit, man," Jackson laughs but there's a nervous edge to it. "I won't." He's got dirty blond hair and a hipster-folk vibe. I could easily take him in a fight and maybe I will at some point.

I glare at him, releasing him. Then I storm into the kitchen to get myself a beer. Vaughn follows me.

"What's up with you, Travis? We've been trying to get a hold of you. You haven't been answering your phone."

I flick open a can of beer and chug half of it, swiping my arm across my mouth. "I've been busy."

"With what?" He notices then that I'm dressed only in a pair of wet shorts. I'm glad I decided to go for another swim on the way back to the house so there are no … signs. No clues. *None of the cum that was all over us. I miss her.* "Or should I say with who?"

I make the mistake of hesitating. "None of your goddamn business."

Vaughn laughs. "Who is she?" My brother knows me too well. I don't bother confirming or denying. She feels too sacred to talk about.

"What are you even doing here, Vaughn? And why the fuck did you bring Jackson?"

"He has a date out here somewhere. And I've been instructed by Roxie to find out what's going on with you. Why'd you bail out of that interview halfway through? She's pissed."

I don't care if my little sister is pissed. I've been on call 24/7 for my family and my band for three solid years. I need a fucking break. "I had somewhere to be."

I walk out the back door and Vaughn follows me.

Jackson's driving out and rolls down his window. "See you guys later." To me, "Don't worry, Travis, I won't say a word."

He knows I don't trust him.

Vaughn and I check out the barn, which he agrees is a perfect place to film our next video and write our next album. We take a walk around some of the acreage. There are two small cabins set back from the pond that look like they haven't been used in a hundred years. The doors are creaky and the few ancient pieces of wooden furniture are covered in dust.

"Can I move into one of these?" Vaughn asks, and maybe it's a good thing. Maybe he can commune with nature for a while and lay off the booze and drugs. He looks sort of out of place against the backdrop of clean air and green trees with his tats and his cigarette and the shadow-bruises under his eyes. Even so, it's easy to see why he has at least one and more often two girls in his bed every night. There's a thread of vulnerability under my brother's bad-boy-rocker look that drives them crazy. They want to save him.

But I can see the roof of Ruby's house from here and I'm cagey about sharing anything about this place—which has become all about her—even with my brother. "Maybe after the tour's over."

He elbows me. "Damn, boy. You're surly as fuck. This isn't the free-and-easy Travis we know and love. Something—or some*one*—is getting to you. Who is she?"

The afternoon, at this point, feels like it might have been a beautiful dream. If I talk about it, I might break the bubble of my fantasy—which sounds fucked up and it is. But the last thing I want to do is dirty my sweet, *hot* memories of her by talking about them.

"All right," Vaughn laughs again. "You can tell me later. We have some kind of photo shoot at ten tomorrow morning, by the way, and the interview with Rolling Stone the morning after the show. Roxie said if you walk out of either one of them she's skinning you alive."

I'm stuck in Nashville all day and all night tomorrow and half of the following day. We have our second-to-last show of the tour tomorrow night.

Two days suddenly feels like an excruciatingly long time.

THE ENTIRE TOUR sold out ten minutes after the tickets went on sale. The stadium is filling up, they tell me.

After the peace and quiet of the countryside, the crowded dressing room feels claustrophobic.

There's a goddamn party going on in here. I wish there wasn't.

Kade hands me a guitar he just tuned. His girlfriend is standing behind him. She has short blond hair and expensive-looking clothes. I don't think I've ever seen her smile. He seems more relaxed tonight, though, than I've seen him lately. "How's the new house?" Kade's watching my expression. Vaughn obviously mentioned a few things to him. My brothers aren't just my brothers, they're my band and my creative collaborators—which means we spend a lot of time together and always have. Which also means they know me better than I know myself, or at least that's how it feels some days.

"It's good."

He continues to watch me, picking up on my vibe. The very fucked-up vibe I happen to be mired in ever since that little angel stepped into my life in the middle of her million-watt ray of sun.

I was distracted during the interview this morning and I'm not in the mood to play this show. I'm doing my best to let my flask of whiskey loosen me up.

What's she doing? Is she going out? What if people see her? What if she's not there when I get back?

Both my brothers are perceptive and in tune with what's going on in my life, since they're so much a part of it. Kade is almost freakish about it. He's less than a year older than me and has always been good at reading me in ways my other siblings sometimes can't. "You all right?"

"If I can get through this show, I'll be fine."

A couple of groupies come up to me. Their laughter grates against my already-frayed nerves.

One of the girls sidles close to me. She has long dark hair and is wearing a very abbreviated cowgirl outfit. She touches my arm but I move away. I don't want her touching me. Only days ago, I might have invited it. I probably *would* have invited it. She reaches for my hand but I grab my flask and take a sip. I can't handle her touching me right now. At all. My reaction is bizarre but I have to move away. Her cheap perfume is gagging me. I walk over to the corner, to get some space from all the people around me.

Something fucked-up is happening to me.

I want *her*. *Her* hair and *her* touch. That reddish-gold silk and that naked golden beauty in the sun. *Drinking my cum. Covered in it, smiling. The rippling softness of her pussy as she comes against my thick, bursting cock.*

Goddamn it.

I want to do it again. Now.

I try to think about the songs. I go through the playlist in my head and sling the guitar strap over my head. I have twenty-seven guitars—my lucky number—and each one of them has its own sound. Kade knows the line-up tonight and he's handed me the Taylor Dreadnought 110 that plugs in. It's the guitar I took to Ruby's house a few nights ago and I'm glad. Maybe some of her stardust still clings to it.

Fuck, I'm losing it.

Roxie walks in. "Five minutes, Travis."

She eyes me and it's getting irritating at this point. They all see the difference in me and I don't feel like being scrutinized over it.

I try to brush it off and concentrate on the music. I

strum a chord but it reminds me of her. It happens to be the same chord her song starts with. The one we sang together about her moving to Nashville.

I'll take her to Nashville, that's what I'll do. Fuck yeah. I'll give her the moon and the stars.

But first I need more of her. I need to taste her and suck on those sweet little nipples until she comes again. And again.

This is more difficult than I'd hoped. *The way she moved, the way she tasted when my tongue was inside her as she came* … it's fucking breaking my heart.

Roxie and Vaughn are watching me.

"I'm fine," I tell them.

"You don't seem fine," Roxie says. "You've hardly said a word all night and you look … messed up."

I glance at a small mirror hanging on the wall and check my hair. It *is* messed up. My hair's brown but turns blonder when I spend time outside in the sun. Chicks dig my hair for some reason. They're always commenting on it and wanting to touch it. I try to smooth it into place. I'm wearing jeans, cowboy boots and a black shirt.

I can hear the crowd out front, chanting my name. Jackson finished twenty minutes ago and the audience is restless. It's time.

"Let's go," Roxie says. To me, "Keep your head, Travis."

I lead the way. The roar starts as soon as I step onto the stage. I take my place at the microphone. The spotlights are on. Everything's dark except for me in my own circle of light. Some girl yells *I love you, Travis.*

I strum the first chord. The lights go up and the crowd goes wild. The first number is an upbeat hit they all know. They cheer and scream and sing along. The girls in the front press up against the stage. I can see the stars in their eyes as they swoon and sing and try to get noticed.

Tonight, it's all I can do to remember the lyrics. My thoughts are full of hot sunlit beauty and wet summer lust.

I miss her so much it hurts.

10

I LET myself into his house through the unlocked window. It's quiet.

My body feels softly electric with anticipation. I didn't sleep much last night. When sleep finally came, in fitful dozes, I dreamt about him. Sweet, sexy dreams that left me tangled in my sheets.

I'm so in lust I think I might be going crazy.

But I don't *feel* crazy. I feel sure of it. Sun-touched and fiery.

This is what I've decided: I'm going to try to tempt Travis Tucker. I'm going to kiss him again. If he lets me.

I think he might.

Last week, I would've had to confess that I'd had impure thoughts, recite a whole bunch of apologies about it and pray for my sins. This week, I'm about to do my best to entice the most beautiful man I've ever seen in the hopes that he might enlighten me. Give me reasons to write the best songs I've ever written.

I'm blaming it all on the music. And on Travis Tucker, with his devil-green eyes.

Even though I've never done anything like this before, I have a plan. I hope it works.

First, I'll sing him my new song, if he wants to hear it. Then I'll kiss him, now that I know how. I'll suck gently on his tongue. I'll touch him, and run my fingers over his chest. To his stomach. Under his shirt, to that tantalizing line of hair that he let me kiss my way down. Then I'll unzip his jeans and reach into them to caress his thick length with my fingers until he's fully hard again.

If he lets me.

I'm going to give him whatever he wants.

I might even let him … *inside me*. Where his fingers were. And his *tongue*, when he licked me like that, pushing into me.

God.

I feel ready. But at the same time, the thought of him doing more than *he's already done* is a little scary, to be honest. He's *huge*. Rose said it hurt the first time. It's hard to imagine what Travis will feel like inside me when his big cock jerks like it did when I sucked on him. When he comes.

I'm starting to soften again just thinking about it. He's so big. So *hard*. It's impossible not to get turned on when you look at him. *To want to get naked so he can see you.* To want to taste him and lick that rock-hard … *manhood* that's so smooth and hot. The way it leaks a little bead of moisture and sort of pulses when you touch it and touch your tongue to it.

I'm wearing a fitted white sundress and a pair of white lace panties I stole from Rose's shopping. She bought herself some new things for her date a few nights ago. She had a whole pack of them still in their tissue paper packaging so I figured she wouldn't miss one.

When he sees how tiny my panties are, he might get hard again. That's what I'm hoping will happen. I'm pretty sure it will. He seems to be hard most of the time. *All* the time, in fact.

Then, if he'll let me, I'm going to push his jeans lower onto his hips so I can hold him in my hands and play him with my fingers.

I don't have much experience with these things—who am I kidding, I don't have *any* experience with these kinds of things—but he seems to like it when I touch him. His eyes get all dark and he looks at me with that wolfish awe.

Then, if I'm brave enough, I'm going to lift my dress a little and lightly touch the head of his cock to me, so he can feel how wet I always am when I'm with him. If he wants to take off my panties I'm going to let him. Then he might push it into me a little. And a little more. I haven't told him yet that I'm already on the pill, but I will. So it's okay if he pushes all the way into me, and spills all that warm, milky liquid inside me. I hope he does it. I want to feel him, big and slick and powerless to resist me. I want to know what that *feels* like. I'm going to do everything I can think of to tantalize him.

I hope I can.

I may not be worldly but I feel different today than I ever have. Like I hold the key to the universe.

I can't wait to see him.

While I wait, I do what he asked me to do, even though it seems like a strange thing to be paying me for. He seemed almost irritated by it last time, that I'd cleaned instead of practiced. So I've brought my music. I'll keep the lyrics calm and abstract, but *I* know what they mean. They're all about feeling your own enlightenment happening to you in real time.

I sit at the grand piano. I let the music trickle through my fingers, where it comes to life. I play another song. The one I started hearing after I woke from the dream I had about Travis last night. It flows easily and I play it all the way through, singing along.

The sun is high now, streaming in the big windows. I play for hours, writing everything down. I have sixteen songs now that I just need to keep refining. By the end of the summer my songs will be polished and I'll have money in my pocket. I'll have experience too. I won't be a *virgin*, for one thing, I hope. You don't show up in Nashville ready to take the world by storm without knowing a thing or two about your own brimming sexuality, that's what I figure.

If I get a chance, I'll sing my new songs for him later. I wasn't sure what he thought of my singing the other night. He was a little hard to read, after we sang together. He stopped strumming his guitar and just stared at me for a while.

Damn, it's hot.

I'm sweating and my skin feels flushed.

I could go for a swim but I want to be here when he gets home. He might think I've left. I wonder what time Travis will be back and I remember what he said. He was so intense about it: *Wait for me.*

I decide to take a quick shower, to cool off.

Humming, I climb the grand staircase. I go up the two flights of stairs to the master bedroom. I don't think he'd mind. I've already cleaned it and gotten his room ready for him.

I wish I knew a little more about him. I know that he's sort of arrogant and thinks of himself as in control of everything. Around other people, I bet he is. He has a softer side too, though, and this is the side that kills me. It's like I've reached past his defenses or something. Like he couldn't say no to me even if he wanted to. It's sweet. And sort of … irresistible.

I can't wait. I crave him with an intensity that's making me reckless. I want to make him feel good. To entice that sexy half-smile he can't hold back when I say something or do something he wasn't expecting. I want to run my fingers through his hair again. And kiss his lips.

He kisses with his mouth open. He always wants to put his tongue in my mouth. It makes me feel hot-blooded and beautiful and fiercely alive when he does that. Then again, pretty much everything Travis does has that effect.

I open the French doors to his balcony and glance out at the view over the rolling, tree-covered hills. I go into his bathroom. There's a towel where I left it for him.

I take off my dress and panties and hang them on the towel rack. Then I step into the shower and turn it on. It's the fanciest shower I've ever been in. Tiled in glossy black and white squares. There are nozzles not just overhead but also coming out of the sides of the shower, like a car wash. One day, when I get a record deal, I'm going to have a shower just like this. And a beautiful house with lots of rooms. And a grand piano.

I let the cool water wash over me. As I turn, the nozzles spray little jets out of the sides of the shower. They caress my body in all kinds of crazy places. Even Travis's *shower* is an erotic experience. The water drips down my breasts and off my budded nipples in little rivulets. One of the soft jets hits me right *there*, between my legs. As I rinse, I let it center there. I start to get warm, tingling lightly. *God.* I gently tilt my hips, letting the warmth build. I touch myself, fingering my silky folds of my body. I remember what his tongue felt like, licking me there. *Sucking on me.* I'd never imagined anyone doing *that* to me. Or how good it would feel, when he put his fingers and his tongue inside me.

The jets are making me a little wild. If I stand here much longer, those pleasure waves are going to happen again. I wonder if it's possible to die from it: from this strange, sweet kind of longing. I want him so much.

Then I hear something. Heavy footsteps. The bedroom door slamming.

Oh my God, he's here.

Travis is home.

He's walking into the bathroom.

He opens the door of the shower.

11

—————

TRAVIS

Four hours earlier ...

"You're number one on the billboard charts. Every song on your latest album has hit the top ten. All four of your albums have gone platinum. You've won six Grammys. The song you wrote for the City Lights soundtrack got nominated for an Oscar and the role you played in the movie—as yourself—was greeted with critical acclaim. Your latest tour has sold out to record crowds. As if that's not enough, your band was voted Sexiest Brothers of the Year by People magazine and you were featured on the cover of Rolling Stone not once this year, but soon to be twice. Tell me, Travis Tucker, where does the magic come from and where can I get some?"

I'm sitting here being interviewed—yet again—by a

138

team of journalists. They wanted to interview us individually this time and I'm last.

This is what it's like when we tour and I can usually handle the non-stop schedule and the never-ending barrage of questions.

Today, though, I'm seriously about to spontaneously combust from frustration and a kind of rage I've never experienced before. If it wasn't Rolling Stone I'd be long gone by now. And how the fuck am I supposed to answer that?

"What's next?" he says. "Another movie? Another album? Both?"

The movie was more of a cameo. All I did was play a song and pretend to order a drink at a bar. "We have another tour coming up in a few weeks. Then we're taking some time off and we'll spend some of it working on our next album."

"There's a rumor going around that you've bought yourself a house outside of Nashville with a barn you plan to record in. Is that true? And where is it?"

No doubt about it: I'm going to beat Jackson Cole to a bloody pulp the next time I see him. "We're planning to record the album in our Nashville studio, where we've recorded the last two," I bluff. It's not exactly a lie, nothing's been decided yet.

"Will it be a departure from what you've done so far, or are you sticking to the magic formula?"

"I don't know yet. I won't know until I write the

songs." Probably not the answer they were looking for but I can't bring myself to care. I'm being feasted on by a swarm of publicity-vampires who won't rest until they've bled me dry, that's what this is starting to feel like. Until there's nothing left of me but a bleached pile of bones. It's not something that's ever bothered me before. But it's bothering me now.

I barely slept last night. We played a long show since it's our home crowd. We got swarmed on the way back to the warehouse. Groupies pounded on my locked door the rest of the night.

I know exactly what the fuck is wrong with me and the whole thing is pissing me off.

That naïve little farm girl with the sun-kissed face. With the hair as soft as silk. With the voice that could break your heart and the body that could make you lose your goddamn mind.

Why *her*? How is it that *she's* gotten under my skin when so many others have tried and failed? And so goddamn easily. I have movie stars coming on to me. I have rock divas and influencers and supermodels sneaking into my dressing rooms.

I shouldn't be so goddamn *hooked*.

She's like a sweet, golden magnet, pulling at me. All the fucking time. It's seriously messing with my head.

"When will the next album be released?"

What if she's not *there*? What if she gets tired of waiting for me and *leaves*?

I know where she lives. I'll go to her window. This time, I'm sure as hell not going to leave her sitting there on that bench with her moon-bright eyes and her soft pink nipples and her skimpy little nightgown that's just asking to be ripped to shreds. This time, I'll scoop her up and carry her home with me. Straight to my bed where I'll feast on—

"Travis?"

"Sorry, what?"

"Could you play your newest single, right here in the studio? We've got enough material for the interview."

I'm relieved. The interview could have been stilted and awkward but I save it with the song. I'm singing to *her*, and it's one of the best acoustic versions I've ever done. Everyone in the room claps and there's a live feed of it with an audience. They want me to take a few questions from fans.

The first chick breathes out her question. "Will you marry me, Travis? I love you so much."

"Sure," I say because I'll tell them what they want to hear, but in my heart I feel almost stricken.

You're too late. I'm a mess, and I'm taken.

Once I get her out of my system, I'll be fine. Once I've had her—*tasted every inch of her and had my fill*—it'll cure this weird, savage addiction that seems to have taken over my life. Then I can move on.

I hope.

Somehow, I already know it won't be enough.

I'm driving way over the speed limit. Good thing my goddamn car corners like it's on rails because I take a hairpin curve and barely manage to stay on the road. *Shit,* I'm going 120.

I could have had her already, when we were on the rock by the pond. When she was pressed up against my cock as she came. I could have easily positioned her and slid inside all that slick, snug nirvana all the way to the hilt. She would have been willing, mostly. Now I wish I had. Maybe then I wouldn't have this hard-on that's become a goddamn permanent fixture in my life. People probably think I've started stuffing my jeans with socks or something. The problem is, the package is real and fully-loaded and ready to fuck like a maniac. I'm so hard I feel like my lust is leeching into every part of me, reaching deeply into dark corners of my twisted-up soul.

I'm almost home. I'm later than I thought I'd be. Roxie cornered me with some studio offer for our next album that she thinks we should consider, with a new label. The money's ridiculous. But I told her I'd need to think on it and today's not the day.

I pull into my driveway, screeching to a stop in a huge cloud of dust. I slam the door of my car and walk to the house in ground-eating strides.

I go inside.

She's here.

I can feel her.

I can *smell* her. I don't even think she wears perfume, but she's in the air. That fresh, sunny whisper.

She's not in the kitchen.

I go upstairs and I can hear the shower running on the third floor. I take the steps in threes.

She's taking a shower.

I go into the bathroom.

And open the glass door.

I kick off my boots and somehow remember to take a few things out of my pockets. I step into the shower. I don't care that I still have all my clothes on. Because she's here and she's naked and wet and simply the most beautiful thing I have ever fucking seen. Her breasts are full and mind-blowing. Her eyes are wide and her eyelashes are spiked with water in curled designs. Her lips are soft and parted. She smiles shyly. But there's more than shyness. She's happy to see me. I fall to my knees and hug my arms around her and rest my head against her thighs. I don't remember ever feeling this *relieved* or this good.

Just being near her is so damn comforting to me I can hardly stand it. *She's safe. She's with me now. I'll kill for her. I'll do anything.*

This lust is fiercer than anything I've ever experienced. It's clawing into me, digging deeper than I can ever remember anything digging.

Her hands are on my head. Her fingers gently weave into my hair.

"Travis," she says softly and I look up at her. "You're here."

The perfection of her face makes my chest ache. A sprinkling of golden freckles. Pale pink lips. Her long, shimmery hair hangs almost to her hips in dripping coils. Tiny rivers cascade from her breasts like she's some sort of otherworldly nymph.

All I can do is sort of stare up at her like a besotted wretch.

"I missed you," she says.

And there, so close to my *mouth*, is her pink, candied pussy. She's not just wet from the shower. She's plump and glistening and *ready*. For me.

Help me.

I *have* to do it: I kiss her pussy and just about black out with my desire for her. She's as sweet as nectar. My cock is a hot, rigid inferno. This has gone beyond passion into something else altogether. Need. Raging desire. Obsession.

Gently, slowly, yet with all the greed of a starving man, I hold her hips and lick into her, sucking on her clit, eating into her until she's moaning. She's got fistfuls of my hair and I *love* this. I'm hers. I want to be hers. *All* hers.

I lick lower, deeper, but I can't get as deep as I want. She's standing, so I turn her around. "Lean over," I growl and she obeys, putting her hands on the tiles and widening her stance to give me what I want. She's offering herself to me in a way that's making me more fucking feverish than I already was. She leans forward and arches her back for me and I thrust my tongue into her pussy as I finger her clit, rubbing gently, working her pleasure. I lick her everywhere. My tongue touches the cove of her ass and she squirms but I hold her there, licking in time to the play of my fingers. I suck on her clit and she comes for me, crying out my name. The sweetest sound I ever heard. I can feel the rippling compressions of her body, the soft, fluttering rhythm. I wait for the waves to begin to calm. Then I turn her to me.

The look in her eyes kills me. It's not manic adulation, like I'm used to. It's a quiet, vast tenderness, a beauty that's the most addictive pull I've ever known.

I stand up and kiss her soft mouth. "I missed you so much, baby." I sound like a love-struck fool. I don't give a fuck what I sound like. I only care about telling her how I *feel*. I want to tell her how important she is, how rare this feels. How monumental.

"I couldn't wait until you came home."

"I came as soon as I could." I pull my soaked shirt off.

She stares at me with wide eyes. She always seems sort of amazed, like she's not used to anything about me. "How was work?"

This makes me smile. She's making polite conversation. "Work was fine. But I couldn't concentrate. All I could think about was doing this." I lean to lick her nipple. I take her breasts in my hands and I suck a taut peak into my mouth. I feel like I'm drinking from her, a spiritual, sexual sustenance that calms me and makes me start coming a little. I'm so close. I suck harder, playing her nipples with my tongue and my teeth. "That feels good," she coos, and the edge of shyness almost sets me off.

"I want to make you feel good. Let me make you feel good."

I take off my jeans. She sort of gasps when she sees me. How hard I am. How fucking engorged and huge and painful my life is right about now. My ten inches could quite possibly have become eleven or twelve under her influence.

"Will you let me wash you, Travis?"

"I'll let you do any damn thing you want to me, darlin'."

She takes the soap and tentatively runs it across my chest, working up the suds. She washes my shoulders, my arms. I just stand there and let her.

She's washing my stomach.

I'm so close I feel like I need to warn her. "Ruby, baby. I'm probably going to come real hard and very soon. You have some crazy effect on me, sweetheart. I'm not usually so ready to fire away but I'm in agony over here and there's no way I'm going to be able to hold on to this."

Control has never been a problem for me before. *This*

is different. I'm about to come. As soon as she touches me, it'll be all over.

She's smiling lightly. Her hands are little slippery miracles. "I *want* you to come. I like touching you. I want to make you feel good."

"You are, sweetheart. You are."

Her hands are on my thighs now. She's playing me. Avoiding the bullseye, making it last.

God have mercy on me.

She cups me in her slippery grip. She's *exploring* me, as though she's spellbound.

Then, her hands ease over my cock. She slides her soapy fists up and down the length of me. It's an agony-ecstasy so extreme all I can do is watch her. The ecstasy is gathering, deep and low. I feel alight with it. On fire. Like I'm not just about to come but also about to die.

"Is this all right?" she asks shyly.

I can only groan an answer, and she increases her pace and the force of her grip until I can't handle it. A wrecking ball of pleasure erupts within me and I'm spurting hot cum all over her hands and her breasts and her stomach in thick jolts. It just goes on and on. I have to close my eyes tight and grit my teeth just to deal with it. I have never come so hard in my life.

She's still rubbing me gently and I almost tell her to stop. It's too intense. But I don't. Her hands are infinitely careful, unbelievably soft. I can *just* cope with these deli-cate caresses, which prolong the orgasm. My cock is still pulsing, still trickling and spasming with the last of my release.

It takes me a few seconds to recover.

Her hands are still on me, smoothing the water across my body to wash off the soap and the cum.

I take her hand and turn off the shower. I grab a towel and dry her hair. I have this desire to do it carefully, gently. I do my best to control the beast that's raging inside me. All it wants is to *get inside*. To take her and own her and worship her with my body.

I dry her neck, her breasts. I use my thumbs and my fingers to play her soft nipples until they begin to bead. *Fuck me, she's gorgeous.* I dry her stomach, her legs. Very gently, her soft pussy. By this time I'm already on the rise again and now she's drying me.

"There's something I want to tell you, Travis."

She sounds serious and I stare at her, wary. What the fuck? She has a boyfriend. She's a Russian spy. She's emigrating to Australia tomorrow and never coming back. Since none of those scenarios seem at all likely except maybe the first one, which I could deal with by beating *him* to a pulp while showering *her* with every affection and gift known to humankind. Then again I don't want to piss her off, or end up in jail. I'll think of something, though. I'm up for the challenge. I'm so damn up for it she won't know what hit her. She'll *never* be able to refuse me or resist me. "Let's hear it."

"I'm on the pill," she says.

She's on the *pill?* That's *good* news. Or is it? *Why* is she on the pill? Has she banged every redneck between here and Nashville? Did I misread her? I'm never wrong about shit like that. And, I realize, the thing is: I so badly *want* her to be a virgin. I feel like fucking killing someone. Or having a goddamn tantrum. *I* want her, now and forever, all to myself.

My sanity is in serious question around this girl.

I need to calm the fuck down.

"Okay," I say, and I do sound calm. A lot calmer than I feel. Then I ask it before I can stop myself. "Why?"

She laughs a little. "Why do you think? Gigi said they only have to *breathe* in our direction. It happened to Scarlett and almost to Rose and there's no way I'm letting it happen to me. I've got plans. I've got things to do and the last thing I want is to get stuck here. I'd go crazy if I couldn't go to Nashville and sing. I'm not willing to let anything or anyone get in the way of that."

I feel my angst and also my amazement affecting my expression. There's a lot to unpack here. "*They* only have to breathe in your direction?"

"Yeah."

"Who's they?"

"You know … men."

"Which men?" I'm in danger of punching my fist through a wall. "Are you …" I almost can't bring myself to ask it. " … getting some wild action around town?"

She looks up at me, her gold-amber eyes flicked with a

hint of mischief. "No. I mean, I haven't been in danger of it before … until … well, now."

I can't help myself. "Ever?"

"No, of course not, Travis. Not even close."

I'm so relieved I feel almost light-headed. We're still standing here, and she's holding the towel, drying little drops from my chest. And lower. My erection has fully revived and is so hard—once again—by this point it's standing straight up and touching my stomach like it wants her attention. It does. So she has to hold it and pull it away from my body to finish drying me. She runs her fingers along my length and I sigh a little: a low exhale that sounds like an animal's growl. I notice then that the bathroom—and everything else—looks all tidy and clean. She's cleaned it. This barely registers.

"Why not?" I blurt out. "I mean, how the hell have you not been chased relentlessly by every man within a hundred mile radius?"

She smiles. She's got the tiniest gap between her front teeth that makes me want to kiss her again, to lick her mouth, to trace along the line of it with my tongue. "I told you. I was at boarding school."

"You didn't have vacations? Or weekends?"

"Not very often. I guess that was the whole point of keeping us there, under lock and key. We had summer school in the summers and community service on the weekends. We weren't allowed out alone. No TV. No internet except for approved websites." She shrugs a little.

"So I'm totally in the dark about the latest pop culture trends, I've watched Netflix exactly twice, and I've only been out of the state of Tennessee once—for ten minutes. But now that I'm free, I plan on fixing all that up as soon as I can. That's another reason I'm going to Nashville. To live my life. To get started."

She's got this defiant little gleam in her eye, like she's already visualizing all the living she's got planned once she gets there. My chest tightens. *I* want to be there, it occurs to me. I want to be with her as she's doing all that. Watching movies and discovering the world and listening to music and finding out about new artists (we'll get to that one soon enough) and meeting people and traveling the world. *I* want to be the one to show her, and guard her from all the men that will want to charm her and use her and keep her for themselves.

They can't have her.

She's mine.

"I just have this feeling it'll work out for me. You know what I mean? You ever get that feeling about anything?"

"Yeah." I have. I knew that feeling once. I was sure, too, when we were just starting out. I was sure I could make it with my talent and my drive and there was nothing on this planet that could've stopped me. I don't tell her this. She still doesn't know who I am and I'm not quite ready to lay it all out yet.

"What about you, Travis? What made you move out to the country? Where did you move from?"

I'm not going to lie to her, I've decided. Ever. But it's true I'm enjoying her total ignorance about the whole fame thing. It's refreshing. "I … have another house in Nashville. I live there when I'm not hanging out here."

She contemplates me, but there's nothing: none of that grasping I-want-what-you-have neediness that colors it. "Wow," she says. "Maybe we'll see each other sometimes."

We're going to do more than see each other *sometimes*, I want to say.

I'm tempted to do it right now. To tell her she can stay with me, at my apartment in the city, and we'll take it from there. But that might overwhelm her. Sure, we're naked, we've gotten each other off a couple times and we're working up to what promises to be one hell of a fuck, but it's probably too soon to be asking her to move in with me. Even so, I almost do it.

"Travis?" She's turned hesitant again and I can't have that. I want her laughing, and playful. "Can I ask you something?"

"Of course you can. Anything you want." I scoop her up and she squeals a small laugh that makes me harder even than I was before. She's so small compared to me. I could dominate her so easily, physically. Problem is, she's already got me wrapped around her little finger. I'll do any fucking thing this girl asks me to. It almost shocks me how invested I am in whatever's happening here, already.

I carry her over to the bed and set her down. I lay

down next to her. My hard-on is jutting out like an elephant in the room but the fact is we've been naked together practically more than we've been clothed together. We can handle it.

"Will you … ? I mean, I don't want to go to Nashville like this."

"Like what?"

"Totally in the dark. About everything."

"I bought you a present," I tell her.

"You did?"

"Yeah. Do you want it now?"

She blinks at me curiously and the soft sweep of her eyelashes slays me even harder as I resolve to buy this girl everything in the world just so she'll keep looking at me like she is right now. "Okay."

I jump up and go into the bathroom. I grab the gift I got her. I walk back into the bedroom and hand it to her as I lay back on the bed, folding one arm behind my head as I watch her.

"You bought me a phone?"

"Yeah. I want to be able to keep in touch with you. So I can make sure you're working on your music when I'm not here."

She turns the iPhone over in her hands, like she has no idea what to do with it.

"I had it loaded with some of the apps you'll need to start recording and uploading your songs."

"Travis," she breathes, like I've just given her the keys

to the universe and answered all her prayers in one fell swoop. Which maybe I just have. "How do you turn it on?"

This makes me smile. My naïve little farm girl is very naïve indeed. In some ways I wish I could keep her here, just like this, and shield her from all the things she's about to discover. I can already tell that would be like trying to cage an exotic bird. What I'm going to have to do is to figure out how to keep her as she flies. *By getting her to fall in love with me.*

I take the phone from her and show her how to swipe up and unlock it. Her eyes light up when the home screen appears. "I'm going to give you a lesson about how to do everything you want to do with this thing," I tell her, taking the phone out of her hand and setting it on the bedside table. "Later."

"Thank you, Travis."

"You're welcome, Ruby."

"I want to kiss you," she whispers. Then she inches closer to me, leaning lightly against me with her thigh touching me and her breasts like two scoops of pale perfection.

"Then do it," I say, challenging her with my eyes. She's shy. She's inexperienced. And she's horny as fuck. It's an absolutely lethal combination.

Very gently, she touches her lips to mine. I let her do what she wants, kissing my mouth in tiny little hesitant nips.

"Give me your mouth." My voice is low and husky.

She does and I weave my fingers through her hair, keeping her in place, kissing her harder. I plunge my tongue into her mouth, which she strokes gently with her own. As she does this, my cock surges against her stomach, gushing pre-cum. *Fuck, this girl gets me hot.* I'm about to come again, already.

"Can I touch you?" she whispers.

"If you don't, I'll go insane."

She smiles and runs a single finger over the slit of my cock, swirling my pre-cum over the crown. "Does that feel good?"

Jesus Christ. "Yeah, darlin'. It sure does."

She's still swirling her fingers over my cock but she's looking at me sort of soulfully. "I feel safe with you. I don't want you to think of it as anything more, though, okay, Travis? I'm not expecting anything from you. We don't have to get all serious or anything. We can just have some fun and you can teach me."

Everything about this girl is new to me. She wants me to fuck her, divest her of her virginity, then watch her walk away. A hot virgin on the pill with no strings attached. Anyone would think it was heaven on earth but there's more than a little cloister of uneasiness to the offer. I don't want to just sleep with her then let her go. My caveman is getting all fucking *possessive*.

"Have you done this ... many times before?" It's

curiosity in her tone, not jealousy, and here's a first: I wish it was.

What to say? "Uh … yeah, a few times." I don't bother telling her I've never done it without a condom. I've never trusted anyone enough for that kind of intimacy. Now, the thought of sliding into her with no barrier between us makes me feel like taking her *right now*. "But never, ever with someone as beautiful as you." I wish I hadn't said that. It sounds cheesy as fuck.

The thing is, I actually *mean* it. I mean it so much I wish I could make her understand how much.

"Who knows what will happen down the road … but I was wondering …" She hesitates, and I tuck a strand of her hair behind her ear.

I kiss her lips. "Ask me. Anything you want."

"You don't have … anyone else? Like, a girlfriend? I guess I probably should've asked you that … before we went swimming."

"No. There's no one else. Of course not. I wouldn't be here if there was." I'm no choir boy but I'm also straight up about what's what. I don't cheat, not that I have anyone to cheat on. I've never been interested in anything long-term. I've been totally focused on my music. I never wanted to get distracted.

Until right now.

And as I'm saying the words, I find I mean them. "I'm yours, angel. Only yours. And you're mine. You're all I can think about, since that very first time I saw you."

Her cool fist is gripping me softly. She's rising onto her knees like she's going to ease herself onto my lap. I can see her pink, wet pussy as she moves. And if I don't take control of this situation immediately I'm going to lose my cool.

God help me.

What I need to do is to make her so happy and give her so much pleasure, she won't even think of going to Nashville without me. I'm going to make such hot, sweet love to her, she'll never want to let me go.

12

TRAVIS LAYS me back onto the bed. He's outrageously strong and it's fascinating to me, again, the differences between us. The strength and shape and size of his body. His bronzed, hair-dusted hardness against my pale softness. The brimming need in him that he's holding back, but barely.

Some buried feminine instinct *likes* that he can pin me down and do anything he wants. I can't stop him. And even though I don't want to stop him, the thought gives me a quiet, primal thrill. Which is strange, when you think about it. The simple biology of this. The deep, voracious cravings of my body. For *him* and his aggression and the liquid gush of his pleasure. I want it inside me. I want to inspire it and make it overflow.

I know I can. Very easily. Just by offering myself to him. Just by inviting him and letting him in. He can't resist me, I can sense this and it's a heady twist, to fully realize your own sensual power over someone so much bigger and stronger than yourself.

Travis lays me against the pillows. Then he crouches over me and kisses my mouth. I try to reach for him but he takes my wrists and pins my hands above my head. He holds both my hands in one of his. His grip is so absolute and the crouching cage of his body so heavy I know I could never escape him. I'm at his mercy and this excites me. I *want* him to dominate me.

"Are you sure about this, Ruby?" His voice is a husked growl. "Because we can wait if you're not ready. There's no rush."

I don't want to wait. My sense of adventure has kicked into high gear. As for my newly awakened libido … well, *she* has a mind of her own and I'm squirming against his big, hard male body. To feel more. *His giant cock is so close. I want it. I want to rub against it and make him come.* "Please, Travis." God, the nuns would freak if they could see me now. It almost makes me even crazier. No one can stop me. This is between me and Travis and no one else. This is ours.

"All right then, baby." His lust has thickened his accent, like it does when he's this hard and this hot. "Relax now. Lie back and let me do everything I want. I'll take good care of you."

The truth is, I know what to expect, sort of, but not entirely. Nothing can really prepare a girl for something like this. It's just one of those things in life that you have to experience entirely for yourself. I'm glad it's him. I don't know him very well, but how well can you ever know a person? Especially when you're on the cusp of flying into life with your wings stretched as far as they can reach. I'm not looking for ties or a relationship. What I want from Travis Tucker is his beauty and his stunning, blazing masculinity. I want him to change my life with it and break me wide open.

"I want to make this perfect for you, but I'm in charge. I want you to trust me to decide when, and how. We're not going to rush this."

He's staring down into my eyes and I nod a little. So he's even bossier in bed. I like it. And I'm pretty sure I can handle him, bossy or not.

"I don't want to hurt you but this will hurt some, since it's your first time. I'm going to get you nice and ready for me now, sweet girl."

I already knew it was supposed to hurt the first time, Rose and Scarlett told me. I'm not scared. Not with Travis. I know how my body reacts to him. I already came for him in the shower and my pussy feels like a warm, blooming flower. "Do it," I whisper.

The fall of his hair over his forehead shades his eyes but I can still see the deep bottle-green glow.

"I'm about to do as much as you can handle, darlin', when I'm good and ready to. I'm in charge here. *I'll* say when." I smile a little then. Because immediately after his macho-man pronouncement, he kisses me, like he can't resist me another second longer. "And how." His dark look is touched by that almost-smile. "And where." But in his kiss I can feel his surrender, his total commitment to taking care of me, in every possible way. Physically, he's in total control, we both know that. But I have a power, too, and I can feel it. A feminine allure that's so strong and so enticing to him, I can sense the limits of his control. *That*'s why he'll dominate me and set the pace. So he can hold on, and come only when I have.

This makes me want to tempt him even more. He's still gripping my wrists and I struggle a little, wanting to touch him and tease him. To test him. To see if I can make him come before he means to.

But Travis won't let me budge. His grip tightens and he deepens the kiss, sliding his tongue into my mouth. I suck his tongue gently, arching my body up to him.

He makes a low, savage sound, kissing me until I'm flushed and lust-drunk. My whole body feels slippery and nubile. I relax into my obedience then, knowing that he won't give me what I want until I obey him and stop trying to fight him or provoke him. He can feel my submission and he loosens his grip, kissing along my jaw, biting the soft flesh of my earlobe gently between his teeth. His hands wander along the skin of my neck and my shoulders, to my breasts. I lay still, praying he'll continue. I'm breathing more heavily now and my breasts rise and fall. I'm so wet I can feel a trickle of moisture tickle the high skin of my thigh. His hands are stealthy and strong and slow.

I *need* him. I need more.

"*Please*," I hear myself murmur. "Please put your mouth on me."

For that he'll make me wait. He smooths my hair, then his hands brush along my stomach, teasing me, tickling me lightly, returning to my breasts only after he feels he's tortured me enough. He's watching my face, challenging me. And when I make no sound, he rewards me. His rough fingers trace slow circles around my nipples, drawing closer. And closer. My nipples are so taut and so sensitive that when he finally touches me, I gasp. He twirls and gently squeezes my nipples between his fingers until I'm moaning and my pussy is pulsing along with each rhythmic pull.

Then he leans down and takes a nipple into the hot fire of his mouth. His teeth gently bite into my soft flesh as his fingers play. Sensation rises and feeds the soft spasms that start low in my belly and surge in clenching bursts. I come, just like that, with only the touch of his mouth and his fingers on my breasts.

"That's my girl," he murmurs. "My sweet, beautiful girl. Fuck, you're sweet."

How does he do *that so easily?*

Travis feasts on my breasts, one then the other, prolonging the swell, until I feel like I'm riding some kind of orgasmic high. He kisses a line down my stomach, licking into my navel, which makes me squirm. Then he moves lower. I can feel his hot breath and I know he can see how ready I am. I lace my fingers through his hair, needing something to hold on to. His hair is thick and soft.

"You're so wet for me, baby. You want me to kiss you and eat that sweet pussy 'til you come again, don't you, darlin'?"

He's asked me the question so I think it must be okay to answer him. I whisper my reply. "Yes, Travis. Yes."

But he doesn't kiss me right away. With his fingers, he traces along the lips of my pussy, opening me, dipping his fingers inside me. He continues his gliding caress, circling my clit. When his thumb skates over the hyper-sensitive bud, my inner muscles start to spasm lightly. I'm almost coming again, but he's playing me, making me wait. I want him to do something, *anything*. To put any part of himself on me, in me.

He licks me, and I moan. He's teasing me with small, careful flicks of his tongue. Dipping, circling. The swell is building. Promising an impossible high. When it breaks, I wonder if there'll be anything left of me.

His mouth suckles on me, but he's carefully avoiding a rhythm.

And then, he presses his tongue against my clit.

It's coming. I'm so close. *I'm so close.* I need to get there. I need … *oh, damn him!* Just as I'm about to come, his mouth is *gone.*

But then I feel his touch again. He's crouching over me, holding his huge, hard cock, guiding it. He's touching the broad crown to me, pushing barely inside.

"*Sweet Jesus*," he groans and his words are half-slurred with lust. "You feel so damn good, baby girl."

I try to arch against him but he's holding me down. His cock slides further into my silky tightness. He forces my legs further apart, pushing deeper. The zinging pressure is dazzling, the thick glide like nothing I've ever felt in my life. "*Travis.*"

"You ready, darlin'?"

Am I? *Oh, God.*

"You ready for me, baby?"

"*Yes. Yes.*"

He rubs his thumb against my clit in a light, rhythmic glide, and each time, he pushes his cock deeper into me, only to draw out, then push back in, wetting his big cock with our juices. There's a burn with each thrust that eases into a sweet, warm ache.

"Oh, fuck, you're so tight, baby. You're so damn gorgeous."

He thrusts his thick, silky shaft deeper. It *hurts* but the shards of pain push the pleasure higher. And higher.

There are tears in my eyes. Because this is real and it's *intense.*

Travis is kissing me as he pushes his cock deeper inside me. *It's so freaking big.* He wipes my tear with his finger. "Hey."

"*Please don't stop,*" I breathe.

"I couldn't even if I wanted to, sweet darlin'."

Travis kisses my mouth, thrusting into me with a brutal plunge. I cry out and grip him tighter. He swears and his head drops a little like he's fighting for control. I know he's all the way inside me now, as deep as I can take him.

Travis holds himself still. His weight on me is heavy. I'm pinned under him, impaled by him, as close to him as it's possible to be.

His mouth is close to my ear. "You all right, honey?"

"Almost," I whisper.

He exhales a small breath of laughter that's laced with something close to agony. I get the feeling he understands what I mean. I want him to make me come again. Like this. I want him to fill me with hot bursts of his cum.

This feeling, of being so thoroughly possessed, is strangely amazing. He's *mine.* He's *in* me. I love him there. I want to keep him there.

"*Hell, Ruby,*" he groans. "Come with me, darlin'. Come with me."

"I am," I breathe. "I am."

He kisses me, dipping his tongue into my mouth in time with his measured, aggressive drives. The pain is sort of excruciating but the pleasure entwines around it, sprouting little wings that push me over some crazy peak of sensation as he strokes inside me with his big cock, again and again, shattering me with thick jolts of ecstasy.

My pussy clenches around him in tugging pulls, until I can feel the warm jets of his seed filling me, spilling, until we're spent and entangled and perfectly in tune.

IT TAKES a while to come down from all that. I feel dazed, and peaceful. He's still on top of me, still wedged deeply inside me. When I open my eyes, he's watching my face. He's so handsome, with his dark emerald eyes framed by dark lashes, his perfect lips and the shadow of stubble across his jaw.

It's the strangest thing, to just gaze into another person's eyes. So incredibly connective. I find myself wondering about it: what it might be like to keep him, somehow, as I follow my path. He has a house in Nash-ville. Maybe we really *could* meet up sometimes.

"You feel like heaven when you come," he says softly.

"So do you," I whisper.

He kisses me and it's a whole-body kiss I can feel everywhere. In my heartbeat. Deep inside me, where we're still wetly locked.

Travis rolls us over, so I'm lying on top of him. I'm reminded again of how strong he is. "Sing me a song," he says.

"I wrote some new ones," I tell him. "For you."

"You did?"

"Yeah."

"I want to hear them."

I sit up a little, and I can feel his cock start to swell again, inside me. I'm sore, and it reminds me of everything that's happened and how profound this is. As I sit up a little more, a trickle of milky liquid wets my thighs and I see that there's blood there too.

I feel different. And I like knowing that no matter what happens to us, I'll always share this bond with Travis Tucker. A bond of blood and beauty.

I'm glad I chose him. And I'm glad I'm not a virgin anymore. Already, I feel like my world just got bigger and more layered. More infused with detail and emotion. I can remember this for the rest of my life, how beautiful it was, and is. I'm going to write a song about it the very first chance I get.

"Go on." He's waiting for me to sing. I hesitate, not because I think he won't like it. I hesitate because I'm savoring the moment. I'm committing every single detail of it to memory.

His hands are on my hips, his thumb barely touching the center of me.

It seems weirdly natural, this intimacy. Almost familiar, already. Maybe because the very first time we saw each other, the experience was so raw and so hot, it sort of blistered through the usual barriers. It feels good, and right.

He's lazily swirling the wetness of our lovemaking, playing my pleasure unhurriedly. It makes me happy, that I'm his. That I'll always be his in this way.

I think he might be fully hard again. I'm straddling him, sitting up. He's filling me completely, like he's a part of who I am. Little flicks of pain and pleasure outline his immense bulk inside me. I know that if I start to move, I could come again very easily. But I want to wait. First I want to see if he likes the song I wrote for him.

The way he's touching me distracts me for a second, but I think through the notes, remembering the lyrics. And I start to sing.

13

TRAVIS

I'M IN LOVE, that's all there is to it.

Ruby is singing to me and making love to me at the same time. My senses are being bombarded with ten types of beauty so intense I'm having trouble processing it all. She's swaying along to her own song and the effect while she's riding my cock is somewhat mind-blowing, to say the least. The tips of her long hair sweep lightly across the skin of my stomach. Her breasts bounce a little as she moves and she's just so damn lovely. Her eyes close when she sings certain notes and I can feel her emotion not only through the music but through this channel of our hot, wet physical connection. I'm so close to coming it's taking everything I have to hold on. I don't want to come again, not yet. I want this to last. I want to ride this high forever, just watching her and listening to her and feeling her.

As for the song, I don't even know what to say about that right now except that she's some kind of goddamn genius. Her voice has a clarity which is simultaneously husked with a colorful edge that's hard to describe. Like she's singing more than one single note at a time. The tune itself is memorable and original, but I can also pick her influences. Weirdly, *I* might be one of them. My song that's currently number one on the charts is somehow featuring, very subtly, in the harmonies.

That she's looking into my eyes as she sings and clenches around my almost-bursting cock is making the whole experience not just physical but somehow spiritual. Like our minds and our souls and our bodies are all entwining at the same time.

She starts the final chorus and I hold her hips as I thrust gently, at first. I play her clit lightly, drawing on her pleasure, insisting. I can feel her tightening around me. She sings the last note and she exhales a soft moan as I meet the gentle writhe of her body with a heavy thrust. She writhes again, and so do I. She's riding me and, *fuck*, she's coming—and those beautiful spasms grip me so fucking tightly the orgasm rockets out of me in excruciatingly intense bursts. I'm filling her with my hot cum. I own her and she owns me. I am so addicted to how this girl *feels*, it hurts my heart.

She collapses onto me and we lay there like that, panting and dazed.

After a few minutes, she lifts herself off me, wincing a

little. I slip from her body and I already miss her. Her thighs are wet. There's a sheen of sweat on her skin and her glorious hair is wild. And I have never seen anything more exquisite in my entire goddamn life.

As she lays next to me, her amber eyes are soulful. I almost regret the new depth there. Of things I've given her and things I've taken away.

I get up and go into the bathroom, wetting a towel. I go to her and gently clean the blood and my own cum from her body. I get this weirdly perverse satisfaction knowing some of it—a lot of it—is *inside* the soft, outrageous beauty of her. My essence is part of her now. I can't remember ever being this gentle before, or wanting to be.

"Did you like the song?" she says quietly.

"I fucking loved the song," I tell her. I mean it too. What I *don't* quite tell her is so close to the surface I have to make an effort to hold it back. Is she ready? Am *I* ready? Three words I haven't spoken since the day before my mother died, and they meant something a whole lot different then than they do here and now.

I'm already formulating a plan in my head.

How did this happen?

I love her.

14

"Hɪ, Mᴏᴍᴍᴀ."

"Hi, honey. Where are you?"

"I'm still at the house next door. I'm staying the night here. There's no one home so I'm going to practice the piano for a while. I've made up a bed for myself in one of the guest rooms."

"Are you sure that's a good idea?" I can hear the workings of her mind. She's wondering if I'm lying to her. She doesn't like that I'm still fantasizing about pursuing my dream of becoming a performing musician. She doesn't want me to be alone here, if that's the truth.

I *am* lying to her, of course, but only because I don't want her to worry. I've already made my choice. And I happen to know my mother ran away with my daddy when she was seventeen years old, against the wishes of her parents, who finally forgave her only after she was married, living in a nice house and had just given birth to a beautiful baby girl. So whatever I do is still going to be more tame than that. At least I finished high school.

She knows I know this. She also knows I've done my time and if she tries to control me, it'll only backfire. Gi is the only one of my sisters that worries about our mother's boundaries. The rest of us are too headstrong for that. Which is probably the reason she sent us to boarding school in the first place. "If you're sure, honey."

"I'm sure."

"Where's the owner?"

"He has another house in Nashville, he said." That part's true, at least. There's no need for her to worry. Besides, it's not like I can tell her the whole truth and nothing but the truth. *Well, Momma, I'm on the pill and right now I'm lying naked in bed with a gorgeous hunk of a man who's older and far more worldly than I am, who's educating me by the second, who has taken my virginity—very thoroughly—and whose hungry mouth is latching onto my nipple as we speak. His green gaze is lazy, challenging me, and his giant cock is getting hard again. I've only known him for a couple of days but I've already had sex with him several times. I've drunk his seed and let him come inside me because I wanted him to. I'm dirty and wet and I've never been happier. Oh, and I'm moving to Nashville.* Sparing her the details is the kindest thing I can do for my mother tonight.

"Chase called. He's left three messages."

"I'll call him back tomorrow or the next day."

"All right, honey. Call me if you need anything."

"I will, Momma." I end the call by pushing the red button, like Travis showed me.

"You'll call who tomorrow?" he asks, biting my nipple gently with his teeth until I laugh and push him away.

"My best friend. His name is Chase. He lives in Oregon. I haven't seen him in four years."

"You haven't seen your best friend in four years?"

"No. He moved. And I went to boarding school."

Travis moves down my body, kissing a trail along my stomach, pushing my legs wider. He languidly kisses my pussy, eating into me with slow gusto like he's found his happy place. "Looks like you've got a new best friend."

His eyes watch my eyes as he licks me. I'm sore and I'm glad he's being gentle, mostly. I ache in places I didn't even know I had muscles. I'm new at this but … is he jealous? I might be teasing him, just a little, when I say it, to see what he'll do. "He wants me to come visit him."

His eyebrows knit together as he gets greedier. His rough beard rubs against my tender, sensitive flesh.

"*Travis.*" I push at his head but he's hard to dislodge.

"What did you tell him?"

"I told him I couldn't come."

I can see this pleases him. His mouth turns tender and he suckles me sweetly. I let him do it, grabbing fistfuls of his hair as he coaxes me into another deep, rippling climax. "That's good, baby," he murmurs against me. "Because I've got plans for you. I need you here."

I'm going with this for now, because I want to. But I'm not sure what will happen tomorrow, or next week. He seems almost possessive of me, already.

I've made up my mind about one thing, though. I can't get paid by him. Not now. That would just be completely wrong. We both know he was making up a job for me, to play his piano for a hundred dollars an hour or whatever. But now that we're having sex non-stop I don't want any blurred lines.

The problem is, I really *do* need to earn money. "I'll stay tonight but I'll probably need to go home tomorrow."

"To call Chase?" He moves, laying his big body over me, positioning himself. He slides his thick length all the way inside me and I make a sound that's halfway between a sigh and a moan because it hurts *a lot*, but the thick, slippery, star-studded friction tips me into another wave of pleasure-pain that's so extreme, all I can do is let him take my mouth as he fucks me slowly and deeply. My body milks him lovingly. He whispers words into my ear as his cock bucks and surges inside me. *You're mine, Ruby. You're so, so beautiful. Oh, fuck, baby, you feel so good. Like heaven on earth. I'll never get enough of you.* The warm jets of his cum awe me and soothe me.

I'm spent, loose-limbed and sated. My eyes are closed.

This crazy intimacy is the wildest thing in the world. I never expected to discover *myself* as I discovered him.

I also wasn't expecting the he-man jealousy. I could *feel* that he was claiming me, almost forcefully. He was reacting to what I told him about Chase. Making some kind of brutish, masculine point. That I'm *his.* In this moment, I am his. Beyond this moment, I can't think about any of it. I'm too comfortable. Too dazed. *Too full of his throbbing, gushing manhood.*

His strong hand holds my face gently as he kisses me. "Ruby?"

I can't open my eyes. I'm sleepy and replete. "Yeah?"

"I want you to come with me to Nashville tomorrow."

This gets my attention. I open my eyes. "Nashville?"

"There are some things I want to show you."

"What things?"

"You'll see."

I almost give him some line about maybe I will. But I don't. Travis Tucker already knows me well enough to realize at least one thing: that's one offer I'll never refuse.

"PLAY ANOTHER ONE."

Travis and I have been in bed all night and most of the day. I've done things with Travis Tucker I didn't even know a person *could* do. He slept with his big body wrapped around me. *Inside* me, when I could take it.

There's hardly been a moment when we haven't been connected or touching or his mouth or hands haven't been holding me and tasting me. There's not a single part of me he hasn't touched or licked or *been inside of,* and it feels strange now, how used to him I've already become. How fast this has all happened and how good he feels.

"Play number one," I tell him. He's been showing me an app that plays music. It's the one he's going to help me upload some of my songs to. He's playing me a few of his favorites.

"We'll get to that one soon," he says. "First, listen to this one."

The French doors of his bedroom are open to the balcony. He cooked me a late lunch and we sat out on his patio and ate it. Then we showered together. Now we're back in bed. I'm laying in the crook of his arm with my head resting against his chest. I watch him as he scrolls on the phone he bought me. The brawny textures of him still amaze me. The steely, rippling hardness of his muscles as he moves. The dark hair on his tanned chest and his arms, which always piques my basest urges. His corded neck and the little pulse that plays, where I wanted to lick him that night he came and sang to me in the moonlight. I love it that now I can lick him whenever I want. I run my finger along the stubble of his square jaw and he gives me a slow smile. I love his quilted abs and his perfect cock, which lays sort of half-mast and innocent-looking against my stomach, sticky with his cum. His thick hair falls in an off-handed sweep across his forehead. His green eyes are pale and colorful today, like sea glass. He's so handsome, I feel a quiet surge of longing, or maybe it's happiness, as I watch his face. His outrageous masculinity is just so *beautiful* in the golden summer light. There's no other word for it.

He hasn't mentioned Nashville again and I haven't asked him about it. This day has been magical. We're enjoying just basking in each other too much to rush it.

His phone rings from the bedside table. It's been pinging all day and he's mostly ignored it.

After around seven rings, he reaches over and picks it up. The screen says *Kade.*

Travis answers it. "Hey."

Because I'm practically lying on top of him, I can hear his conversation. When I try to roll away to give him some privacy, his arm wraps more tightly around me. "Where are you?" I hear Kade say.

"I'm not going to get there until later."

"Travis, we were supposed to tune up at five and run through a couple of things. What's up with you never answering your phone when every one of us has been trying to get a hold of you?"

"I'm sure you guys can handle it without me. I'll be there around seven thirty."

"We start at eight, Travis."

"And I'll be there at seven thirty."

I can hear Kade sigh. "You owe me one for breaking this news to Roxie."

"She'll survive."

"When are you going to introduce us to the mysterious stranger you've gone AWOL all over?"

Travis exhales a laugh. "Soon enough."

"All right, brother. See you at seven thirty and not a minute later."

"Sure thing."

Travis ends the call. I can see on his phone that the time is 5:03. It's much later than I thought. This day has gone so fast. "Who's Kade?"

"My brother." He's still cagey about telling me too much about his life. I figure he'll tell me when he's ready. Or when I manage to ask my questions into a perfect donut hole of opportunity.

Like now. "Who's Roxie?"

"My sister."

"What's happening at eight?"

Travis uses the sheet to wipe my stomach. It seems strange all of a sudden that I have no idea what he does. Especially after all that's happened over the past few days. "I'll tell you all about it on the way. We should get going in case we hit traffic."

"To Nashville?"

"Yes. To Nashville."

"What do you have to tune up for?"

"I have a show tonight and I want you to come."

"A show?" *He has a show?* "What kind of show?"

"I'm a singer. And a guitar player and a songwriter." He gets up from the bed. "Come on, darlin'. I didn't realize it was already five."

How do I not know that he's a performer? One that has a *show?* "You're a musician? *That's* what you do? Why didn't you tell me?"

He's all casual about it but I'm starting to get the feeling I've missed something big, and important. "I did. I showed you. I came to your house and sang to you."

He walks into the bathroom and grabs my clothes, which he brings to me.

I get out of bed and pull my dress over my head. "Is the show in Nashville?"

"Yes." Travis puts on a pair of jeans and a shirt. He brought his bag up from the car earlier. He pulls on some cowboy boots. "Let's go."

I follow him down the stairs and out the back door to his car. It's some kind of extremely fancy race car. It's blue with two white stripes. "Wow. What kind of car is this?"

"It's a Shelby GT350." He opens the passenger door and grins at me. "Jump in, baby. I'm going to take you for a ride."

Before I know it, I'm driving along with him at a hundred miles an hour, straight toward Nashville.

He smiles over at me as he shifts gears and I have to remember to breathe, he's so gorgeous, with his dark-bright eyes and his thick hair. With his warm-looking tan and his muscles straining against his shirt. My stomach does a little flip as I remember *gripping* those muscles. *As he thrust his big, spilling cock into me. As we came together.*

He seems to read my mind. "After the show I'm taking you back to bed."

"I should probably call my house again."

"We'll stay in Nashville tonight."

"If you hear me lying, it's only to save my mother some grief," I tell him.

He gives me a look that starts me going again. I feel the delicious soreness as my body responds and remembers. "I'll never tell," he says.

Rose answers. "Hi, Rose. It's me."

I hear her sniff, like she's been crying again. "Ruby, where are you?"

"I'm at the neighbor's house. Remember? I got a job as a cleaner."

"Oh, yeah."

"I'm going to stay here tonight. The owner's not home and it's a big job, so I might as well keep going."

"Are you sure you want to stay there alone?"

"Yeah, I'll be fine. Are you okay, Rose?" I ask, even though I already know the answer to that. Rose's love life has become predictably unfulfilling when it comes to getting her boyfriend to commit to anything.

She blows her nose. "He hasn't called, even though he

promised me he would. Even after everything that happened."

"He's probably just busy."

"He's always too busy for me. And you know what, Ruby? He told me he *loved* me and I believed him. That's how stupid I am."

"It's not stupid to give someone the benefit of the doubt. I'm sure he'll call. Everything'll be okay. You'll see." But my reassurances sound empty. If his track record is anything to go by, most likely he *won't* call. Most likely he'll disappoint her over and over again until whatever's left of their relationship crashes and burns. Now that I actually understand how hard it is to resist temptation, I can relate to Rose's sorrow even more. I wish I could track down that jerk she's so in love with and slap some sense into him. Rose might be a drama queen but she has a beautiful heart. "I'll see you tomorrow, okay? Tell Momma I'm fine."

"I will, Ruby. Bye."

I end the call.

Travis glances over at me. "Everything okay?"

"My sister's boyfriend is … well, he isn't very reliable. He keeps telling her he'll call but he never does."

"What an asshole."

"Yeah."

Travis is gripping the steering wheel as we drive fast along the highway. The sunset is dazzling tonight, painting the sky with swirls of orange and pink as the sun touches the horizon. "Ruby?"

"Yeah?"

"What we've done means something to me. I promise to be honest with you, okay? I'm not going to do that to you. You need to know that."

"It means something to me too, Travis."

It's reassuring, I guess, to hear him say that. I hope I can believe him. It was never my plan to have a relationship before I got my career going, ever. And I don't know how to define this thing that's happening between us, which seems to have all the momentum of a runaway train. It scares me a little, how good I feel when I'm with him. How addicted to his presence I've already become. I love how beautiful he is. I love how his softer side shines through his cool swagger like he can't help giving me anything I want. How the grip of his strong, tanned hands as he drives reminds me of his uncontrolled ecstasy, of how that grip feels on my body when he comes hard.

There's far *too* much to love about Travis Tucker.

"While I'm being honest," he says, "there's something else I want to say to you."

I'm remembering how his rough stubble felt when he kissed the high, soft skin of my thigh. I'm getting wet just thinking about the things he did to me with that wicked mouth.

But then he says, "Ever since I saw you that day, playing

my piano in the sunshine like a golden angel, I literally can't think of anything else. I'm fucking obsessed with you. I thought making love to you would get some of this fever out of my system, but it's only made it a million times worse. The thought of anyone else even *looking* at you tonight makes me want to kill someone. And now that I know how damn good you feel and taste and—*fuck*." He glares at me almost angrily. "What I'm trying to say is that every time I think about you—which is all the damn time—I want you. What I really want to do right now is pull over and take you into the back seat so I can rip off those little white panties with my teeth, get you on your hands and knees, eat you until you're dripping wet and then fuck you from behind until you're moaning and coming hard around my big cock. I want to fill you with my hot cum. I want to know you're all wet with it while I'm out on that stage, where I'll be losing my mind because I'm not next to you, protecting you and kissing you and telling you how beautiful you are."

I'm staring at him and he stares back. He glances occasionally at the road, then meets my eyes with an arrogant, challenging sneer. I don't even know how to react. But my body does. His crude delivery has lit some fire in me that wants to be fed. He's challenging me. He thinks he's so tough. I'll meet his challenge, damn him. I'll meet every challenge he gives.

"You're a big talker, Travis Tucker," I say softly. "But the thing is, I'm *already* wet. For you. For that big cock you keep going on about." I reach over and run my palm over his button fly. *Wow.* Under his jeans, he's rigid and huge.

His eyes are crazy-dark and I wonder if this might be dangerous but I don't care. I ease my hand over his hard length, fingering him.

"Fuck, Ruby."

I feel the swerve of the car as he pulls over into some parking cove. It's darker now and I'm glad. Especially when he pulls to a stop and opens his door to jump out. Before I know it, he's around at my side, hauling me roughly into the back seat, where I crawl in on my hands and knees. I look behind me and the buttons of his jeans are undone and *holy God*, his cock is enormous and hot-looking and shiny at the tip.

He pushes up my dress and rips down my panties. "Goddamn it, baby girl. You drive me so crazy." He leans in, licking me in greedy strokes, flicking his tongue against my clit. He forces my legs further apart, pushing his tongue deeper. I arch my back and offer myself to him. I let him do whatever he wants. He sucks my clit into his mouth and I almost come, but then he's moving, climbing over me and I can feel the plump head of his cock sliding against the slippery lips of my pussy. He positions himself, and I hear his low murmur. "You like it rough, darlin'? You want me to fuck you real good?"

"God, Travis. Yes."

He thrusts all the way into me, burying himself to the hilt.

I cry out as he takes me. But the pain of each thrust glides into a mind-blowing pleasure as he drives his thick cock into the slippery constriction of my body, over and over.

He plays my clit with his fingers as he thrusts again and *oh God, it's happening*. I'm arching back against him, rocking and meeting each drive. "You feel too damn good, baby. Let me feel you come."

I'm there. I'm at the peak and the rushes start, tugging tightly around him. I can feel his cock pumping gushes of his liquid heat, flooding me in hot throbs as he comes hard.

Reality feels hazy. All I can feel is him and this rippling, feral pleasure.

The waves calm.

Slowly, he pulls out of me. Rivulets of his cum wet my thighs. He uses a t-shirt to clean some of his seed from my body. "I'm going to know I'm dripping down your leg as I sing tonight. You're mine. I don't want to let you out of my sight. I don't want to share you with anyone."

"I don't want to share you either," I whisper. I didn't really mean to say that. I guess it's okay to be honest, though. That's how we've decided to do this.

"You don't have to share me, sweetheart. I'm yours. I'm so far gone I can't see straight. I can't see past your golden glow."

He helps me back into the passenger seat of his car as he kisses me. *I'm so crazy for him*, is what I'm realizing. I don't even *want* to be this crazy for him. Travis Tucker is getting under my skin, that's what's happening here. With his big cock and his killer smile and all that wild pleasure he gives me every chance he gets.

Travis's phone rings in his pocket. "Shit." He stuffs himself back into his jeans. "Let's go, baby."

He jumps in and starts the car. His phone starts ringing through the radio system. The screen says *Vaughn*.

"Hey, Vaughn."

"Where the fuck are you, Travis? We're on in ten minutes."

"I'm running late."

"No shit. You were supposed to be at the stadium three hours ago."

Stadium? "I'm almost there."

"Roxie's having a fucking conniption. Jackson finished half an hour ago. The crowd's getting restless."

"Just tell them I had car trouble."

"You drive a brand new *Shelby*, Travis. We all know there's nothing wrong with your goddamn car."

"I'll be there in ten."

"Just hurry the fuck up."

Travis ends the call.

"Who's Vaughn?"

"My other brother."

"Is he in your band?"

"Both my brothers are in my band. My sister is our manager."

It's not long before we're driving into the center of Nashville.

"Things will probably get a little crazy tonight," he says. "Stay close to me, okay? You'll have to wait backstage while I'm on, but I want to be able to find you when I need to."

"Okay." It's sort of sweet how over-protective he's being. I mean, how crazy can it be?

WE DRIVE into the stadium and the parking lot is completely full. It's starting to hit me that this is all for *him*.

He's performing as the headline act at the Nashville stadium to what appears to be a sold-out crowd. I guess in hindsight, the clues have been getting more and more obvious, but I just never imagined such a thing.

Travis Tucker isn't just famous, he's a *superstar*.

All the gatekeepers and security people know Travis's car. They wave him through.

I suddenly feel like I need a lot more information. But we're pulling up at the back entrance and a crowd of people wearing back-stage passes and security badges and headsets are swarming around the car. Travis's door opens and they pull him out. People are yelling and talking and trying to usher him away. He literally has to fight them off to come around to my side of the car. I'm almost afraid to get out. But Travis wraps his arm around me and holds me close to his body and we're led by his entourage into the back-stage area of the stadium.

It's busy and chaotic.

Everyone wants Travis.

Someone must have told the crowd that he's here because a huge roar goes up from inside the stadium.

We get to the backstage area and I can see the crowd. A huge, colorful mass of humanity, yelling and cheering. This stadium holds seventy thousand people. I've never seen so many people together in one place before in my life and it's daunting, imagining what it might be like to *sing* to that.

And I can't believe all this is for him and, after everything, all the songs we sang and the wild intimacy of our bodies and our minds over the past few days, he never *told* me. "Travis. Why didn't you—"

But I'm interrupted by a pretty dark-haired girl, who storms up to Travis and grabs the front of his shirt with her fist. "I'm literally going to *kill* you." Then her gaze slides to me. And to the way Travis's arm is very protectively looped around me. She stares at Travis, then at me.

"Roxie," he says. "Meet Ruby. Ruby, this is my very understanding, calm and reasonable sister, Roxie."

"Hi, Roxie."

I can definitely see the family resemblance, in the shape of her very-blue eyes, which are watching me with a hint of wariness. "Nice to meet you, Ruby. And by the way, I'm none of those things. I'm an irate and stressed out mess and it's all his fault."

"Actually," Travis drawls, "it's Ruby's fault." He grins down at me and I feel myself blush. *As a trickle of moisture drips down my thigh.* Travis's gaze is sort of hot, like he knows this and is happy about it.

Two men approach us and—*wow*—they look a lot like Travis. They have the same tall, muscular build, that straight-to-the-gut X-factor. One is dark-haired with a lot of tattoos and the other one has longer hair and incredibly blue eyes. They're both gorgeous. And they're both staring at me like I just flew in from outer space. Their gazes sweep all the way down to my feet then slowly back up again. Considering I was locked inside a glorified convent not even a week ago, it's sort of dizzying to find myself *here*, with the brawny arm of an ultra-sexy rock star slung possessively around me as his two hot brothers check me out, no doubt noticing how flushed and wild-eyed I am from the outrageously enlightening events of the past few days … *including the lingering endorphin rush of my most recent orgasm and the tickling slide of Travis's cum dripping down my leg. Yikes.*

"*Now* I get it," says the dark-haired brother. "I'm Vaughn," he says to me. "This is Kade."

"My brothers," says Travis, still holding me close to his body, as though he doesn't want them getting too close to me. "Ruby Hayes."

"Hey, Ruby," says Kade, as he hands Travis a guitar. "We thought he'd been kidnapped."

Fresh heat warms my face because they seem to all know exactly what Travis and I have been up to for the past two days straight and they're intrigued by me, the mystery stranger who's kept him hidden away. They watch me with that same wariness as Roxie did, though, like they're assessing my motives when it comes to their brother.

Even with all this going on, I need to know. I'm angry that he kept something this huge from me. I glare up at Travis's face. "Why didn't you *tell* me about this, Travis? It didn't even *occur* to you to tell me who you actually *are*? That you're some big shot famous *superstar*? After everything we've talked about? Why would you leave that out? Why did you do that?"

"Because I didn't want it to get in the way," he says.

"In the way of what?"

"Of how you felt about *me*. Without all the hype. Just me."

"But—"

"I *liked* that you didn't know who I was. It meant that you weren't after me for the things everyone's always after. The money and the fame. I wanted you to want me despite those things. Without those things."

"Of course I wanted you for you, but you could have *told* me."

"I would have. I was about to. I was waiting for the right time."

"Travis," someone says, interrupting us. But I glance over at his family, who are all watching our exchange with interest, and I see a different expression on their faces now, like I've just reassured them about a detail they were wondering about. An important one. Maybe I've just confirmed to them that I'm not a gold digging groupie who's only after him for his money.

"It's time," one of the sound guys says.

Travis takes my face gently between his rough hands and he kisses me. Deeply. I'm a little shocked that he would kiss me like this in front of his family. "Don't go anywhere, darlin'. I need you right here. Don't be mad at me, all right? I'll make it up to you. Roxie, don't let her out of your sight."

The way they're all watching him and sending each other bemused glances makes me think Travis's behavior is unusual and out of character. "Sure thing, Travis."

Vaughn's eyebrows lift and he gives his brother a sardonic grin. "Shit," Vaughn murmurs, shaking his head as he laughs softly.

Roxie steers Travis toward the stage. "Just go. Go on. Sing your heart out and I'll make sure Ruby is right here when you're done."

Travis kisses me again, more slowly than maybe this moment calls for, then he turns and walks onto the stage, slinging his guitar into place. Kade straps on his bass and

Vaughn steps up to take a seat behind his gigantic drum set.

The crowd goes absolutely wild.

Travis stands at the microphone. The spotlight shines on his hair. Even if I'm still angry that he neglected to tell me some glaringly major details about his life, in this moment, I can only watch him in awe. He looks like a god, with his halo and his tall, lean body. If I ever tried to dream up perfection, it wouldn't look nearly as good as Travis Tucker looks right now.

He strums one chord. The crowd quiets by a degree and Travis starts to sing.

You're my wild, wild girl and I know what you like. Let's go for a ride on a hot summer night.

Holy shit.

It's the song.

The one from the radio. The one I've been humming and using for inspiration and getting turned on by, all this time. Since the first time I heard it.

It's *Travis's* song.

And as he sings it to this crowd of seventy thousand adoring fans, I can hear in his voice—even if I'm imagining it but somehow I don't think I am—that he's singing that song to me.

Got you in my arms, babe, feels so good and so right. I'll hold you close all the hot summer night.

This realization makes my eyes sting. Because I'm in

awe of his talent and his beauty. Because I love the song and the way he's singing it right now.

When he hits the last note the crowd erupts. "Thanks for coming out tonight, Nashville. It's good to be home for our last show of the tour." Girls in the mosh pit are pushed up against the stage, crying and screaming *I love you, Travis* and *Marry me, Travis*.

Wow.

In this setting it's sort of hard to process the fact that he's *mine*. I don't know how far it extends or how long it's going to last—and I swore to myself I'd take the time to discover my own path before I committed to anyone else's. But in at least one way Travis Tucker is mine and he always will be. He's my first. *He's in me*. His essence is a part of me and I can feel it.

And I decide to forgive him. I guess you *would* wonder if a person wanted to be with you because of the fame and the money. I guess he was making sure. One thing I do know is that, if anything, this will make things harder between us. In some ways, I would have preferred to keep him all to myself.

He's mine.

Don't you go falling in love with him, Ruby Hayes.

Maybe I already have.

But that would be crazy. First, I haven't known him long enough to fall in love with him. Second, I'm not a romance-addict like my two older sisters, whose sole mission in life was always to have a boyfriend and get married and have babies and be taken care of. Not me. That was never me. I wanted to take care of *myself,* while meanwhile taking the world by storm.

It's a lot to think about. Especially as I watch him on stage. He was clearly born for this. He's cool and beautiful and his voice is to die for. He deserves every ounce of their adoration.

Roxie brings me a stool to sit on. She's busy with the sound crew but she stays nearby as I watch Travis and his brothers. They're incredibly good. They're real musicians. Their sound is fresh and original while still walking the commercial line. All three of them are dazzlingly talented, with a rocket-fueled energy and a stage presence that could only be described as mesmerizing. It also doesn't hurt that all three of them are also drop-dead gorgeous.

Time flies as they play for several hours and do two encores.

"That's their last song," Roxie tells me.

And then Travis does something I'm not at all prepared for.

"I have to apologize to ya'll for being late tonight," he says to seventy thousand fans, "but I think you'll forgive me when you understand the reason why. I'm about to show you." I see Kade shoot Vaughn a confused look. The massive audience cheers for their idol. At first I think I'm imagining it but then I hear it again. The first three chords of the first song I sang for him, on the bench by my window under a full moon.

"What's he doing?" Roxie says.

"I don't know," I tell her.

But I do know.

Don't do this, Travis. Please don't do this. I'm not ready.

"See, the thing is, I've got a new friend and she has the prettiest voice you've ever heard." Travis plays the chords again. "Ruby, come on out here. Come and sing a song with me."

Travis. No.

"You sing?" Roxie asks.

I can't even answer her. My heart is pounding in my chest.

"Come on out here, darlin'. Don't be shy. Roxie, send her out."

Holy hell.

I'm frozen.

"Ruby," says Roxie. "I don't know what he's doing but I don't think he's going to take no for an answer."

Can I do this?

But then I realize I can.

This is it. My first audition.

So I take a deep breath. I stand up and I smooth my dress. Then I take that first step and keep going.

I walk out to him.

He's smiling at me and has this tender look in his

sparked eyes that makes me almost forget that seventy thousand people are watching me.

A hush falls over the murmuring hum of the crowd. The lights dim except for two spotlights. One on me and one on him.

Someone whistles.

Travis makes room for me at the microphone, lowering it just a little so I can reach it easily.

"This is Ruby Hayes," he says into it. To me: "You ready?"

It's strange: I *am* ready. I feel weirdly like I'm *home*. Like this stage, with him, is exactly where I belong. I nod and he starts playing and we sing the song I sang for him in the moonlight. Our voices dance around each other, entwining in the crazy night. It's the most amazing thing that has ever happened.

When the last note fades, the crowd roars and I look out into a sea of glowing phones, as far as the eye can see. Kade and Vaughn are there and the three of them take a bow.

Travis waves and slings his arm around me. "Goodnight, Nashville. We love you." Then he leads me off the stage to the thundering cheers.

As soon as we're off, we're swarmed. Travis leads me to a waiting tour bus, which will take us to their warehouse, where there's an after-party. The bus is crowded to the point of being claustrophobic and I understand now why Travis bought the house. He once told me he bought it so he could hear himself think and I can see how he would need to take a break from this life sometimes.

He keeps me with him, his arm secure around me, touching my hair, murmuring in my ear. "You sang like an angel. You were so good."

"So were you, Travis. You're unreal."

Vaughn grins at me as he pops a bottle of champagne. He's striking with his black hair and his blue eyes and his ink. "Ruby, where'd you learn to sing like that?" he says, pouring our glasses until they overflow with bubbles. "Rox, you nailed that tour, honey."

"That's some voice you've got, Ruby," says Kade. There's a girl with him. She has short blond hair and a stand-offish vibe. He doesn't introduce us and I smile in a sort of greeting but she doesn't smile back.

"Thanks."

"Have you ever performed before?" Roxie asks me.

"No. That was my first time."

They talk and laugh and I sip my champagne, still reeling from the surreal experience of what just happened to me. What's *still* happening to me.

We get to the warehouse and we're ushered through a back entrance because the street in front of the building is swarming with people. More rabid fans, desperate to get a glimpse of the Tucker brothers.

The warehouse is a huge loft with an industrial, modern look that's been softened with wood and brick and a wall of windows looking out over the glittering city.

It's furnished with expensive-looking leather couches and funky lamps glowing golden light. It's already full of people. A passing waiter serves us more champagne.

I'm already tipsy from the first glass but I figure it's a night for celebrating.

Travis gets pulled into a conversation with some people and Roxie draws me over to the window.

"Do you have a manager, Ruby?" Roxie asks me.

"A manager? No. No, I don't have anything."

"We should talk."

"Sure. I'd love that." I'm sort of shocked by her suggestion but I'm also distracted, because I can see Travis talking to some people deeper into the room. Roxie gets pulled away into another conversation.

It's *so* crowded in here.

Travis is surrounded by groupies. Lots of them. Beautiful, scantily-clad girls who obviously have one thing on their mind: getting as down and dirty with Travis Tucker as possible. They seem open to the idea of *all* getting down and dirty with him at the same time. In fact two of them seem almost as interested in each other as they do in Travis.

One of them grazes the back of his shirt with her fingertips. Another's watching his mouth, like she's thinking about kissing him. A slim redhead with a tattoo on her hip, above her very-low rise shorts, fingers a strand of his hair. They're like sharks, slow and stealthy, circling him.

Travis steps away from them. He's trying to talk to a guy that's sitting on a couch. But the girls are insistent. Their hands graze his shirt and his hair. He turns his back to them, talking to the guy on the couch.

And then I see more clearly who he's talking to.

It's Jack. Jackson, they called him.

Rose's boyfriend.

I've only met him once, as he was picking up Rose a few months ago. But it suddenly all clicks into place. He's a musician. He travels a lot. *Because he's with Travis's band. He's their opening act.* I didn't recognize him on the far side of the stage earlier, with the hat he was wearing and the sunglasses. His hair is longer than it was the last time I saw him.

Jackson is sitting on a couch and there's a girl sitting on his lap. Another girl is sitting on the arm of the couch, leaning over him, playing with his hair. Jack is laughing. He tips back a shot of whiskey someone hands him. The girl on his lap is kissing his face. She's unbuttoning his shirt, running her hands over his chest.

No wonder he's too busy to call Rose.

It's pretty obvious he's gearing up for a big night … and one that very definitely doesn't involve my sister. It occurs to me now that I don't know if Gi got Rose to go to the clinic to get a morning after pill. I never asked her. I hope desperately that she did. I wonder if he'll knock up these girls too. The way his hand is placed under one of the girl's shirts seems like a pretty good clue that he'll take whatever they're offering. Maybe he's got a whole slew of pregnant women crying by their phones across the country, waiting for him to call them.

And suddenly I wonder if Travis does too. This is his lifestyle. He has thousands of women throwing themselves at him every night. Like they are right now.

Have I been a fool … for thinking I was special? Does he feed those lines to all the girls he spends time with?

I remember asking him when we first made love if he'd done it many times. *Yeah, a few.*

How many is a few? A few hundred? A few thousand?

I stand here and the rest of the party sort of fades out as I watch the women fawn over Travis as he takes a long drink straight from the whiskey bottle.

The champagne is making my head spin.

Do I have this all wrong, for thinking he was mine? Do all the rock stars play around? Maybe all I am to him is a naïve country wannabe with the same fantasy as all the girls in this room and all the girls in that vast, cheering crowd.

Travis got jealous when I once mentioned Chase to him. I'm a little surprised now at the fever of my *own* jealousy. I never meant to care so much. I wanted experience. I wanted to know what it felt like to *feel*. Travis sure showed me that. But now I'm starting to realize that all that *feeling* has dug a lot deeper than I expected it to.

It was never my plan to get attached. But … *how dare they touch him?*

He's mine.

And why is he letting them?

Does he tell *all* the girls about his honesty and his big cock right before he fucks them in the back seat of his Shelby?

Ruby, calm down. You're overreacting.

Another girl sidles up to him and whispers something in his ear. He has to lean closer to her to hear what she's saying. She smiles and touches his face.

Before I know what I'm doing I'm walking over to Travis.

He sees me and he makes an attempt to brush a few hands off his shoulders, but they're not easily dissuaded, these girls. They're *ravenous* for a piece of Travis Tucker. What a goddamn gentleman, though, really. To notice me standing there and make some lame attempt to fight off his fans for my sake.

"Hey, Ruby," says Jack. How can he be so blasé about this? He's making no attempt to brush off *his* girls.

"Hi, Jack." I can't help myself. "Have you spoken to my sister lately? The one who's waiting at home for you to call her like you promised you would?" *The one who you confessed your love to before having unprotected sex with and then didn't bother to find out if she was okay.* Which isn't *only* Jack's fault of course, but I don't sound as calm as I was going for.

"Rose knows I have a gig tonight," Jack says, all

laconic smile and sweet innocence. "You sang real good, by the way. I never knew you could sing like that."

"She knows you have a gig, yes. What she doesn't know, though, is that your gig involves getting laid by a bunch of women that aren't her." This isn't really like me at all but I'm suddenly feeling as melodramatic as my sisters. Jack is a stunning-looking man. He has dark blond hair, mischievous dark eyes and a buff, lanky body. I'm thinking about what a beautiful baby he and my sister might have made. "You should have been honest with her."

The girl on Jack's lap shoots a few daggers out of her eyes, annoyed that I'm diverting his attention. "Be careful about believing everything he tells you," I say to her.

"Ruby," says Travis. "What's going on?"

I glare up at him. His jewel-bright eyes and his colorful hair just have this divine way of catching light. I notice again the halo-effect being cast by the lamp behind him and it makes me almost hate him. For being so damn perfect. "My sister believed the things he told her. And now she might be in a lot deeper than she can handle. And he doesn't care."

"You mean … *Jackson* is your sister's asshole boyfriend?"

"I'm not an asshole," Jackson protests vaguely. The girl on his lap giggles and kisses his lips. "Am I?"

"No," she coos.

I need to get out of here. Before I get in deeper than *I*

can handle. Because Travis Tucker is basically better than anything I could have dreamed up. He's also not just the answer to all *my* prayers, but every woman's prayers on the entire damn planet.

Just like Jack was the answer to Rose's prayers.

If I get in any deeper than I already am, it'll hurt me too much when Travis plays me. Because I think I might already love him and I *know* I don't want to share him.

I can admit to myself in the heat of this moment that I'm *already* in too deep. So deep I think I might shatter when I walk away.

I don't want to humiliate myself by crying in front of all these people, so I turn and start making my way through the crowd. I hear Travis call my name but I reach the door and I slip through it. I run down the stairs. I don't know where I'm going but right now I just need some distance. I've drunk two glasses of champagne and I can't think straight.

"Ruby!"

I reach the bottom of the stairs where there's a huge metal door. I hate him, for making me feel *so much*. For giving me more than everything I ever knew I wanted.

"Ruby!"

I try to open the door but it's either locked or too heavy to budge. There's a thick tinted glass pane next to the door that looks out onto the street and I can see that, out there, it's packed with people. I fumble with the lock but Travis catches up to me and grabs me, twirling me around and pinning me against the door. I struggle against his hold but it's unbreakable.

"Let go of me! I'm leaving."

"Ruby, stop fighting me! What are you doing? What's wrong?"

"What's *wrong*?" I hate the sound of what comes out. "True, it's been three whole *hours* since you told me in your car that I was yours and you were mine. That I wouldn't have to share you. Maybe it slipped your mind when your groupies started groping you." I sound like a desperate wretch, the very last thing I ever thought I'd turn into. I was the one who was supposed to be *immune* to all this, the one who was going to control my own destiny and not have it decided for me by something so cliché as love.

Lust, I can handle, I've decided. Love is dangerous. Love will break your goddamn heart.

I can see that, under his concern, there's something else. Amusement, maybe. Or triumph. He's *happy* I'm jealous. And he sounds calmer now. "They weren't groping me." He's holding back a smile, which infuriates me to no end.

"You think this is *funny*? You think this is some kind of freaking *joke*?" And *goddamn it*, why can't I just swear like a normal person? "You let them touch you."

He has the nerve to laugh softly and gaze down at me almost tenderly. "They didn't touch me."

"They *did* touch you! They put their hands on you

and you let them do it." He's so stunning it brings tears to my eyes, which makes me even more furious. Why should I even care about this? We've known each other for less than a week. It serves me right for getting so carried away, for diving into the deep end before I even knew how to swim. "Let me go, Travis. I need some air."

He leans to glance through the thick pane of glass. Then he moves back, pinning me in place again. But it's too late. Girls immediately start screaming and pounding on the door. "If you do that I'll be forced to chase after you, which could be a very sticky situation since there are probably several thousand people out there. They would swarm us and film our little argument. Then the video of me getting down on my knees to beg for your forgiveness would go viral. Is that really what you want?"

I swipe away a tear. "No," I say, surly.

"They follow me around, Ruby, that's just the way this life is. But you're right. Next time I'll tell them to fuck off more persuasively. I don't want *them*, honey. I want you. Just like I said to you."

I hate that I'm crying over this. Over him. "That's what Jackson said to Rose too. This is all happening too fast. I need some time to think, Travis. I need to leave."

"I'll take you anywhere you want to go. But don't go because of *them*."

Can I handle this overload of emotion? I guess that's why they say love hurts. It's physical as much emotional.

My heart literally aches. "I meant what I said. I don't want to share you."

Travis wipes my tear with his finger. "I'm sorry you're upset, honey. But nothing happened. You're over-reacting."

"Like Rose is overreacting? He lies to her all the time."

"Well, I'm not him, Ruby. That's the difference. I told you that. I've been riding this crazy-train for a long time and I'll be honest with you, I've never been exclusive. I've never wanted to be exclusive. I've never tried to be exclusive. But I want to be exclusive now. With you. I want to get exclusive all over you, goddamn it, because your jealousy is hot as fuck and also adorable. And I'm not just saying that because it's what you want to hear. I'm saying it because it's fucking true."

I want to believe him. And I can feel that at least one part of what he just told me is very *much* true because his rock-hard body is pressing against me dizzyingly and his hand is loosely grasping my throat like he'll do whatever it takes to keep me there.

His expression is full of passion and also laced with a hint of vulnerability, which clashes with his superstar, hard-bodied, heart-throb vibe. "Don't you dare walk away from me." He's glaring at me soulfully. "I need you. I'm in love with you."

"You can't be," I whisper.

"I *can* be," he growls. "I *am*." He lifts me and I have

no choice but to wrap my legs around him. He's so damn strong. He holds me exactly where he wants me. "I was in the process of firing Jackson when you got the completely wrong impression back there. I've been wanting to get rid of him for a while because I've never been a fan, for several reasons. I'm going to talk it over with my family. But we'd already decided to hold a few auditions for a new opening act for our next tour. It's twelve shows and I want you to do it. I want you to come with me. I want you to move in with me. Now. Tonight. We'll spend time out at the new house and we'll spend time here at the studio. We'll record your album and you can perform your songs on tour. We're going to do this together and you're going to trust me because I'm giving you my word that I won't lie to you. I can't guarantee that everything will be perfect 24/7 for the rest of time. But I want to try. Because I'm crazy for you and I'm in love with you."

My brain can't quite process the deluge of all he's offering me. "You don't know me well enough to be—"

"I *do*," he insists gruffly as his fingers push my panties to the side, gliding over my sensitive flesh. I go instantly, shamelessly wet.

"*Travis.* Someone might see us."

"No one can see us. And you're going to stop fighting me every step of the way, baby girl. You want me as bad I want you. Fuck, you're wet for me. You want my big cock right now, don't you, darlin'?"

That's one thing I can't argue with because he's

unbuttoning his jeans as he rubs my clit and kisses my lips. I do. I want him with everything I have, even if I'm still mad as hell at him. I wrap my arms around him and kiss him back.

His huge cock rubs against my slick wetness. "What are you doing to me, Ruby?"

"Kissing you." I gasp as his thick cock forces entry, stretching me open and sliding deep. He starts thrusting in a fast, in-and-out rhythm that feels so damn good it brings more tears to my eyes. "*Oh, Travis.*"

He puts his hand over my mouth to keep me quiet as he thrusts faster and I moan again even though we're doing it in a public place against a door with a thousand people on the other side of it. The gliding, thick, slippery friction is too much. His hand is over my mouth and we're staring deep into each other's eyes as he fucks me hard and fast. The pleasure is astounding, crashing through me in voluptuous clenches. My whole body is coming, milking his length tightly, over and over. He swears and clenches his teeth as his release explodes, pumping his hot cum deep inside me in seedy bursts until it's dripping down my thighs.

My head is lolling on his shoulder and he cradles me against him. "*Sweet Jesus,*" he mutters.

I vaguely hear voices far above us. Travis pulls himself from my body, setting me carefully onto my feet, tucking himself back into his jeans and smoothing my dress into place. My face is wet with tears. My knees are so weak

I'm not even sure I can stand up without his support. And under my dress I'm literally overflowing with his cum. "I can't go back up there."

He smiles at me, wiping my tears with his thumbs. "You're going to hold my hand and we're going to walk right through that party into my apartment, which is at the far end of the warehouse. I'm going to hold you in my arms all night long. And tomorrow we're going to make a plan. You're going to move in with me and we're going to make your music happen. Together. I'm going to help you make all your dreams come true."

I start to say something. But he holds his fingers to my lips to silence me.

"You can argue with me tomorrow."

It's true. I'm too exhausted to argue with him now. Slowly, I nod.

Travis takes my hand, making sure I'm stable enough to walk. Then he leads me up the stairs, through the crowd, ignoring all the people who call out to him.

He takes me to his apartment, which I can abstractly appreciate is the most sublime space I've ever seen. He pulls off my dress and takes me into the shower, where he washes me carefully. Then he dries me and tucks me into his bed. He wraps his body around mine and I hold him close as I kiss his lips and lace my fingers through his hair.

I'm not sure what I've gotten myself into but this offer is just too damn good to refuse.

Sometimes you have to play the hand you've been

dealt and I guess this is definitely one of those times. I think I just got dealt four aces and a wild card.

I can't know how things will pan out. I'll do my best to survive him.

Travis Tucker has packed more lust, inspiration, heartbreak and love into six days than I've experienced in the entire rest of all my years.

Of course I'm going to go with him.

Of course I'll live with him and tour with him and sing with him.

And make love to him every chance I get.

I blink at him and he smiles in the darkness, all green eyes and promises.

As I drift into sleep, some lyrics I wrote for him weave through my mind.

Tell me where does this road lead and where does it end. Oh, where does this road lead and where does it end.

15

———

"THERE'S something I need to tell you all."

The three of them look up at me.

I'm in the kitchen with Momma and Rose and Gi and we've just cleaned up from lunch and I haven't told them yet that I've packed my one bag that holds everything I own and it's right now sitting next to my bed. Travis brought me back from Nashville this morning. I told him I needed a few hours.

My mother and sisters can already tell that whatever I'm about to say is big. They go quiet, waiting for me to speak.

"I got a job. It's in Nashville."

"What?" says Gi. I'm going to miss her most of all and it's just now starting to hit me that I'm actually leaving.

I take a deep breath because this is harder than I

212

thought it would be. "Momma, I've already made up my mind that this is what I want to do and I'm going to do it so please don't try to stop me."

Momma's face pales a shade.

"You know how I told you someone bought the house next door? Well, his name is Travis Tucker. He's a musician."

"Travis *Tucker*?" breathes Rose. My sisters know exactly who Travis Tucker is. "Jack is in his band." I don't know exactly what the state of affairs is between Rose and Jack right now. I do know, though, that Gi did take Rose to the clinic to make sure she took a morning after pill. Not only that, but Gi insisted she get an on-going prescription so it doesn't happen again because she's sick of worrying about it. I swear Gi worries about whether Rose is about to get knocked up more than Rose does. And if Rose is still with Jack, it's her own fault if she gets her heart broken. I told her about what I saw.

"Well … not exactly," I clarify. "Jack used to be their opening act, Rose. But not anymore. Now …" It almost sounds too crazy. "*I'm* going to be their opening act."

"What?" Rose laughs. "Sure you are. And I'm going to sprout little wings and fly to the moon."

"Ruby," Momma says. "Is this true?"

"It's true. It's a twelve-show tour and they've asked me to come with them. It doesn't start for a few weeks but I'm going to spend time making a record. Travis is going to help me. They have apartments and a recording studio at their loft in Nashville. I'll get paid a lot of money to do the tour and my record's exposure will be huge."

"Ruby, you're too young. You hardly know these people."

"I'm not too young, Momma. I'm exactly the right age. It's what I've been dreaming of since Daddy told me he wanted to see me singing on stage one day. *He* would want me to follow my dreams. You do too, I know you do. This is what I want."

Momma sits down on a chair like her knees have suddenly gone weak. I catch her eye and I want to mention that she was only seventeen when she left home to follow *her* dream. But I don't. She already knows that.

"They'll be here soon. I'll introduce you and—"

"*They?*" Rose sort of clutches herself.

"Travis and his brothers. He thought you might like to meet them since I'll be staying with them and going on tour with the band."

Rose squeals with excitement. "They're coming *here*?"

Just then I hear the growl of Travis's car pull into our driveway. "Oh, look. Here they are."

Rose and Gi rush to the window. Rose makes a sound like a strangled sigh. "*Oh my God. It's the freaking Tucker brothers.*"

I open the door for them and they come in. They're standing there in our kitchen looking wildly … out of place. Huge and tanned and handsome and respectful in their double denim with their colorful eyes and their tattoos and their thick hair. You can practically see the testosterone radiating off of them, like big, lusty animals. Travis is holding a bouquet of flowers and a wrapped present, which he hands to Momma.

"Nice to meet you, Mrs. Hayes," he says and my mother actually blushes. "These are for you."

I make the introductions and Rose swoons when Travis shakes her hand.

It's entertaining to watch.

Momma asks them, "Would you like something to eat?"

Vaughn grins at her. "Yes, please, Mrs. Hayes."

So as my mother starts getting stuff out of the fridge, Vaughn pulls up a chair and straddles it the wrong way around, resting his chin on the back of it as he stares mischievously at Gigi—whose look today (and in fact most days) might be described as hot librarian. She's got her hair up in a messy bun and her black-framed glasses on. But Gi is the most beautiful person I know, inside and out, and she always looks sort of glamorous in a fresh, careless kind of a way.

"Wow," Vaughn says softly, blinking his blue eyes at her.

Which is also entertaining. I can't think of a worse match.

As this is going on, Kade sits next to Rose and studies her gently for a few seconds. Then he says, "You should dump him."

"Dump who?"

"Jackson. He's cheating on you and you are *way* out of his league."

Rose blinks at him. Flags of pink color her cheeks. "He is?"

"Yeah. But you already knew that, right? You must have suspected it."

It takes her a few seconds to respond to this. "I guess I did. And, I mean, Ruby said something about that but—"

"You should find someone who treats you like you deserve to be treated. Like the most important, beautiful person in the world. Don't ever settle for anything less."

Rose looks like she's about to cry. But then she lightly squares her shoulders. "I know. You're right."

He smiles at her as he tucks in to the plate of food my mother just put in front of him.

The three of them basically eat everything in our kitchen.

"This is the best food I've had in a long time, Mrs. Hayes," Vaughn gushes.

Gigi opens the present and it's a new iPad so they can follow me online, Travis tells them. So they can watch the shows and download our music. There are also hotel vouchers and three VIP all-show passes. The three brothers are so charming—and *hot*, who are we kidding—they entirely win over Momma and Rose, even though Gi is a little more stand-offish, maybe because Vaughn spends the whole time watching her.

Then it's time to go. When my mother cries, Travis tells her, "I'll protect her with my life." The pronouncement feels sort of overdramatic in the moment but my mother and my sisters all stare at him with the same expression on their faces: a longing, maybe, for their own promise like that. For a hard-bodied, suntanned, beefed-up man with a fire in his eyes on that same purpose, who might say those words about *their* lives.

Vaughn kisses the back of Gigi's hand in an overdone gesture and she blushes.

What I realize is that, for all their bravado and testosterone, in their hearts these brothers are romantics.

Maybe we all are. Maybe *that's* the meaning of life: finding someone to share it with who will protect you and whisper sweet words to you as they overload you with lust and love and rapture while also taking you on the ride of your life.

I guess I'll find out.

Because before I know it I'm in the passenger seat of Travis Tucker's race car with his two brothers in the back and the radio cranked up. I've got the wind in my hair and I'm on my way to Nashville.

MY LIFE TAKES on a surreal glow.

What I very quickly learn is that a girl can have all the grit in the world but it still won't prepare you for getting swept away by a non-stop, rocket-fueled party with a brigade of hot, high-octane superstars and their insatiable entourage.

The busy warehouse is always full of production crew, staff, groupies, journalists, photographers and an endless parade of people who need or want something from the Tucker brothers. I've never met three people who are so *in demand*. Everyone wants a piece of them.

And soon enough, everyone wants a piece of me too.

When the media learns that I'm going to be the new opening act for the band—which I had to audition for and which they said (somehow, even though I was nervous as hell) I aced—I've now got *followers*. Roxie showed me how to set up some social media accounts and within a day of the news breaking, I had half a million Instagram followers. Then when someone posted a photo of Travis kissing me and it went viral (it's a cool, artistic photo and we look sunlit and glamorous) the number shot up to seven million overnight. The day after that I got offered two hundred thousand dollars to post a picture of myself wearing a particular brand of sunglasses. Which I accepted.

The truth is, the whole thing is sort of overwhelming. All I've ever known is the house I grew up in, my family, our calm, frugal home and my quiet, rigid school life. Here, the hectic activity and noisy, jam-packed warehouse and studio can be daunting, mainly because it never ends. I've never partied before in my life. *Or* worked sixteen hour days. My old life involved classes, prayers and supervised activities like reading and freaking needlepoint. Now I hang out with rock stars and influencers and wildcats whose breakfast consists of cocaine and whiskey. People have sex on the couches. They literally swing from the chandeliers. They're crazy with life and pushing boundaries and spending money—and they have no limits.

What I soon find is that I *need* Travis.

He becomes my rock.

The more I get to know him the more I learn that he's not just beautiful to look at, he's a beautiful soul. He's a turbo-charged hunk in the prime of his life with a relentless sex drive and talent to burn, but he's also patient. He's tough and rough-edged but he has one of those personalities that, at its core, is steady and grounded. And *fun*. He laughs easily and he doesn't take himself too seriously.

It fascinates me that he radiates a rare kind of power. Everyone loves him and respects him. They'll do anything he asks. They want to please him. He's one of those people who, in a different setting, might be a general or a king.

It sometimes feels like I've hitched my wagon to the sun.

And Travis will do absolutely *anything* for me. I don't always understand why.

He finds my inexperience cute and endearing and sort

of beguiling. He notices how I react to things and he's interested in how I feel. He's by my side every second of the day as I record my album, which turns out to be incredibly hard work. I'm as green as they come and the production team gets frustrated with me because I need to be taught *everything*, from how to put on the fancy head-phones to what a sound cloud is. And I make mistakes. Lots of them. I get notes wrong and some of my songs weren't even finished. Which means I have to sometimes improvise on the spot and work late into the nights.

Travis is there for me. He helps me and practices with me and patiently teaches me when there's something I don't understand. Which is ridiculously often.

Angelo, the band's producer, finds all this as tedious as hell, but Travis seems enchanted by it. He *likes* that I need him. He *wants* me to rely on him. Part of him seems to almost thrive on it.

It sometimes concerns me how *much* I need him.

It was never my plan to need anyone. Especially not this much.

To make matters even more tangly, we have outra-geously hot sex every chance we get. And while I can't get myself to entirely admit that, emotionally, I desperately need him … physically, I am *crazy* for Travis Tucker. I simply can't get enough of him.

To say that he feels the same way would be an under-statement.

He says my body is his haven and his fantasy. We

retreat to his apartment many times a day. We make love all night. He's demanding and relentless and such a fierce, beautiful lover that all I can do is *feel* and cling to him as he takes me to the very limits of what I can handle. I drink him and I take him into my body worshipfully. He has so deeply saturated me with his seed and his passion that he has changed me with it. Our bond feels important and necessary. Travis has infused me with his essence so thoroughly, I don't like to think about ever having to go without it. I'm addicted to his body and the pleasure he forces me to take. That part of him, I can admit, I *love*.

The L word, though, is a tiny thorn between us. He's said it to me twice, after knowing me for a week. I haven't said it back and I know he wants me to.

The fact is, I only left home a few weeks ago. I'm eighteen years old and I always thought the road of my life would have hills and bends and unexpected corners along its slow cruise. I don't feel ready to commit to *anything* yet for the rest of time. As beautiful and addictive as he is, if I tell him I love him, it'll lock this into place in a way I'm not sure I'm ready for yet.

He doesn't push me but I can tell … it's a *thing*.

There's another *thing*, too, that irritates Travis like nothing else does.

Chase.

Now that I have a phone, he calls me all the time. At least once a day and sometimes more. He sends me photos. He likes everything I post. I get messages from him constantly and he's become more insistent about reconnecting.

I do want to see him and it's been nice to catch up on more of his news.

But it's the one thing Travis is very definitely *not* easy-going about. Especially when Chase told me he got a ticket to our upcoming show in Portland. Travis has been surly about it ever since he found out.

"Of course he's going to come to the show, Travis," I told him. "He's my best friend. He wants to see me sing."

Travis hates when I call Chase my *best friend*. "How can someone you haven't seen in four years be your best friend? *I'm* your best friend now."

When he said that, I kissed him and laughed at him gently. "You're not my best friend."

"What am I, then?"

"You're my very gorgeous … lover."

"I can be both," he said to me, then proceeded to give me four back-to-back orgasms to prove his point.

My phone rings. It's Chase again.

I've just finished a meeting with the band, the sound crew, the production crew, the lighting crew and the publicity crew about the tour schedule. We're leaving tomorrow morning in a fleet of buses and equipment trucks to drive to Los Angeles. My opening act will consist of eight songs and Travis has helped me perfect each one. All of them are on my album of sixteen songs which is now finished and available for download on all the major music platforms. I'll appear on stage with his band to sing the third song of their first set each night of our tour.

I'm sitting in a chair by the wall of windows and the Nashville loft is, as usual, full of people. Travis is talking to Roxie in the open plan kitchen area and he's distracted. So I take the call.

"Hey, Chase."

"Hey, Roo, how are you? Excited? Nervous?"

"Terrified. But, yes, excited. I can't believe this is really happening. I can't believe I'm actually going *on tour*."

"You'll finally get to see the world."

"In two days I'll be in *California*. I've always wanted to go there."

"And now you'll get your chance. Let's make a plan to meet up after your show in Portland. Can I get a backstage pass or something? I can't wait to see you, Roo."

"I'm sure I could get you a pass. I'll ask Travis."

"I never pictured you with someone like *Travis Tucker*. Wow. I mean, I just think you'll get tired of the age gap and the playboy lifestyle after a while. I keep telling you that you and I are meant to end up together, Roo. You'll see. You need someone who's more on your wavelength. Eventually you'll want someone who *knows* you, like I know you."

Chase is always saying things like this. I don't answer. If Travis happens to overhear, I know for a fact it won't go down too well, to put it mildly. I'm not sure what he would do, but I don't want to test him or provoke him. It's becoming more and more of an issue the closer we get to the tour.

"Ask Travis what?" I hear over my shoulder. I glance up at him and he's as rough-edged and dazzling as always—and extremely pissed-off looking.

Carefully, I say, "Chase was wondering about a back-stage pass," adding—even though I'm not sure why: "He wants to meet you."

"I'll think about it." Travis takes my phone and hits the end button before handing it back to me. "Okay, I've thought about it. The answer is no."

"Why not? That was rude, by the way."

With that, I'm scooped up into Travis's arms and he's carrying me toward his—*our*—bedroom. "I'm going to show you the true meaning of the word rude right now, darlin'."

He takes me to bed, kicking the door closed. He lays me back and peels off my clothes sort of aggressively, kissing my breasts, sucking on my nipples roughly. "*Mine*," he growls, holding me down. He kisses his way down my body, licking my pussy greedily, eating into me and making me squirm with the lewd, hungry delves of his tongue. His coarse-silk hair rubs against my thighs, tickling me. "I don't want him calling you all the time. How many fucking times a day does he have to call you?"

"It's not that many." His scratchy beard rubs against my tender, sensitive flesh and I gasp. "It doesn't matter."

"Oh, it *matters*. A lot. Because you're *mine*."

I get that he's a big lusty alpha male and he's claiming me as his territory or whatever but it's all a little over the top. All I'm doing is talking to an old friend once in a while. There's no harm in that. Travis's jealousy is overblown, that's all there is to it.

I make the mistake of pointing this out to him. "I'm not actually *yours*, Travis," I whisper. "I'm mine." He latches on to my clit and sucks on me as he pushes two fingers inside me, rubbing his other finger over the secret cove of my ass, working every sensual trigger I possess. He sucks my clit, milking strongly as his fingers slide, until I'm *just* about to come. He knows exactly what drives me crazy, but he's teasing me. Punishing me. He avoids a rhythm, making me wait. But by now I'm so turned on I feel loose and reckless. *"Please, Travis. Do it."*

"Then tell me what I want to hear, baby girl. You're mine mine mine and that's the only way you're getting a goddamn thing from me."

Fine. If he's going to be punishing and crazy about it, then I'll torture him right back. I'll make him as crazy as he's making me. I writhe against him, offering myself to him. *"I want your big cock inside me, Travis, please. I'm so wet for you. I want you to fill me up with your hot cum."*

It's one of his weaknesses. He sort of loses his mind when I talk dirty to him.

I hear the clink of his belt buckle as he unfastens it.

"Travis." I reach blindly for him. I want to make him come. *"Give it to me. Please."*

He manacles my wrists with one iron-strong hand. He lays himself over me so his cock slides against my wet, swollen pussy. I try to rub against him and squirm so I can get the broad end of his huge length inside me but he pins me down with his big body, glaring down at me with his eyes dark and his hair falling over his forehead.

He looks mean and dangerous and all I want in this world is for him to *make me come.* "Please, *Travis.*"

"Who do you belong to? Say it to me. That's the only way you can have me. Say it."

I'm fighting him, maybe, because I'm as stubborn as he is.

He parts the intimate folds of my pussy with his hot, thick, slippery length. *Oh, God, I could come right now if he'd just let me squirm against him.* But he holds himself—and me—infuriatingly still. "Don't play me, Ruby. You're *trying* to fucking rile me, aren't you, baby girl? Well, it's time you learned your lesson. Tell me what I want to hear."

I look up into his darkly vivid eyes and I say it. Because it's him and if he doesn't give me what I need right now I'll go mad. It's true, after all, even if I don't know how he did this so easily and it scares me to think about *how* true it is. It's so true it could—*it will*—break me if he ever decides to walk away. But he's here now and I want every inch of him, every heartbeat, every pulse and every sigh. "I'm yours, Travis," I whisper. "Only yours. All yours."

Through his fury I can see that my words spear straight to the deepest part of his emotion. And I realize at that moment as he thrusts his giant, bursting cock deep inside me, instantly triggering a tidal wave of pleasure so severe my body bucks and clenches with the overload, that Travis Tucker *really* loves me. That this big, lusty animal with his hard muscles and his pumping, spilling cock is making love to me *as* he fucks me. His lust and his love compound each other. I can *feel* his devotion, in his need and his desperation, as his release overtakes him.

We come hard, gripping each other as our bodies bond wetly in a slow, grinding frenzy of pleasure.

We lay like that for a long time, letting the ripples calm and ebb. He smooths my hair with his fingers. He kisses my face.

Then he pulls himself from my body in a rush of wet warmth.

For a while he just watches me, staring into my eyes.

"What happened to your father?" he finally says.

I'm not expecting the question. "He, uh, he had a heart attack. Five or six years ago."

"That must have been hard."

"It was. It felt like … he'd left us. We all needed him so much." It's strange to talk about it, but I find myself wanting to tell him. "Scarlett and Rose found their comfort from … well, men. Gigi buried herself in books. I wrote and played my music. It was my link to him. But we were never quite the same."

"I'm sure."

"What about your parents?" I've never heard him mention them.

"They died. Around six years ago."

"I'm sorry."

"It was a drunk driving accident. My father was the drunk driver."

"Travis," I whisper. "I'm so sorry."

"So I get how hard it can be. My parents were always … free spirits. My dad had been having issues for a while. When we lost them, we all dealt with it in our own way. Vaughn got crazy, Kade got quieter and more introspective, Roxie won't touch a drop of alcohol and she refuses to date anyone, and me, well, I cruised past it all. Not feeling much, just gliding along the surface." He weaves his fingers through mine. "Until you. Now I'm feeling *everything*."

I touch my fingers to his face. He's so beautiful.

"It affects you in ways you don't realize," he says.

"Yes. For me, the world got emptier and it also got scarier. We felt like we'd lost our protector. I think that's why my mother sent us to boarding school. So we'd at least have some supervision and some support."

"You must have felt like you needed to rely on yourself a lot more. Like you had to dig in to your own grit."

"That's exactly how I felt. But … I had Chase. He

was there for me when it happened. He helped me get through it. Until he left."

Holy hell. I think I might have just had my first therapy session.

My father left me. And then Chase did.

That was how it seemed to me at the time.

Travis is *getting* me in a way that very few people ever have. His perceptiveness feels wildly connective. *How can he get me and fix me and love me so effortlessly?* Huskily he says, "*I'm* not going to leave you, honey."

My heart skips a beat.

Because he just speared straight to the core of what holds me back.

I'm scared to love him because I'm scared he'll leave me too.

My eyes fill with tears because he somehow just dug up the crux of all the pain and fear I've buried for a long time.

I want to try to explain this to him but he holds a finger over my lips. "You don't have to say anything, Ruby. I understand. I actually *do*. But you should know that it's my mission and my obsession: to convince you that I'm here for you and that I'm not leaving. I love you, baby, so much it's making my head spin. I'm *crazy* in love with you. When I told you I started feeling something when you walked into my life, I meant that. You got under the surface like nothing and no one ever has. The only thing I care about is keeping you safe and happy and close to me. From that very first second, I *knew*. You hit me like a goddamn lightning bolt. And I know all this has happened fast and if you need time, that's okay. But *I'm* ready. I'm fucking *all in,* darlin'. I want to marry you and make music and babies with you and give you everything you've ever wanted. I know that's a lot to take in right now but it's the truth. You can take all the time in the world to figure out whatever you need to figure out. But I'm going to be right here by your side as you do it. I'm not going anywhere. And you're going to give me everything, including that little piece of your heart you keep hidden and protected. That's the part I want most of all."

He holds me as I cry. But these tears are cathartic. The more I let go of, the more exhausted I feel but also, in a different way, strangely stronger too. Tonight, he doesn't ask me for anything more.

I'm going to have to make a choice. I'm either going to have to give myself to him in body and soul with no holds barred, or walk away. And I already know I can't walk away from him. Of course I can't. He's already become as necessary to me as my own lifeblood. Travis Tucker has completely taken over every aspect of my success, my future and my life.

Even worse, he owns my heart. Even that hidden away part. Somehow, he found the key.

Now I just need to figure out how to survive him without shattering or losing myself.

I think maybe I can.

And as I fall asleep in his arms, I realize it's not a hard

choice. Now that he's broken through, I wonder why I ever thought it was.

THE TOUR IS the wildest experience of my life. As he promised, Travis keeps me close to him. We ride the tour bus across Arkansas and Oklahoma, through parts of Texas, to Arizona where we even make a detour to see the Grand Canyon because it's Travis's favorite place. And now mine too. I want to stay longer but we have to stick to the schedule. Travis tells me we'll come back here on our honeymoon, then he gives me a look that's equal parts hot lust and hopefulness and I fall deeper in love with him. Ever since he broke through my realization, I feel like I'm in free fall. I can't slow it down.

And then it's time.

An hour before my first performance, I'm so nervous that Travis and Vaughn insist I do two shots of whiskey. No more, no less. Miraculously, it helps. I guess that's why they call it liquid courage. It takes the edge off my terror of performing on my own for a sold out crowd of 70,000 at the SoFi stadium in Los Angeles. Roxie comes into my dressing room and gives me a hug and a beaming once-over. She helped me choose my costumes. The dress is a short, glam, white little number with sequined fringe that probably cost more than my daddy used to earn in a year.

I touch the cross I wear on my necklace that he gave me and I think of him.

I'm here. I made it. I know you can see me tonight.

I kiss Travis like I've never kissed him—like I *need* him with everything I have—until Vaughn whistles, then I walk out onto the stage and I sing my heart out. When they cheer for me, which is the most deafening sound I've ever heard in my life, I feel like I'm flying.

We do shows in L.A., San Diego, Las Vegas and San Francisco. When Travis hears that my sisters aren't sure about driving such a long way, he charters a private jet and puts them up in some fancy hotel in Seattle so they can see our second-to-last show of the tour. They *love* it.

My reviews have been mostly good. The press latched onto my story, about the naïve country bumpkin making it big. And they can't get enough of my romance with Travis. My downloads are through the roof and I now have thirty million followers. Which is hard to even think about.

It's not perfect, though, and not all the reviews are glowing. Like the particularly brutal one that honed in on one detail that's worried me from the beginning. Namely, that I'm touring with the band only because I happen to be sleeping with Travis.

Travis Tucker's barely-legal girlfriend got the lucky score of a lifetime when she got hired to be the opening act of the Tucker Brothers Band on their 12-show West Coast tour. The girl has talent, sure, but it's unrefined and lacks the superstardom vibe the brothers so convincingly bring to their legendary performances. No offense, Travis, but maybe hire a singing-and-performing coach for your fresh-out-of-the-convent tween girlfriend before unleashing her onto the music scene just because you happen to be enjoying all that in the sack.

I cried, because it was painfully true.

Travis didn't even flinch. "Shit, honey, that's rule number one: never read your reviews. People'll say anything for attention and to get whatever twisted revenge they can on anyone who's more successful than they are. You're here because we want you here."

Or, more accurately, *he* wants me here.

Travis placated me by showing me another review.

The Tucker Brothers Band ups their game with their newest addition to their 12-show Sunstorm Tour, the dazzling rookie Ruby Hayes. Smoky-edged innocence meets a raw powerhouse of talent, delivered in a sultry-sweet package that has audiences spellbound by the newbie's unfiltered X-factor. Definitely one to watch. Ruby Hayes is sure to excite fans as much as she's clearly exciting Travis Tucker.

Wow.

Travis is much more experienced than I am, and he has a much thicker skin. "The best way to prove the cynics wrong is by forging ahead, staying true to yourself and singing your heart out the way only *you* can," he said. "Your voice is beautiful, baby, and so are you. Don't give it another minute of your time."

So I try to do exactly what he tells me to do.

After that, it was Sacramento and Reno.

And then Portland.

Tonight.

I've been too busy to make a plan with Chase. And I've been careful about corresponding with him. On tour, Travis is both fierce and focused. The music and the performances take over everything. He's less relaxed and more possessive than ever before. And I've changed. I'm head over heels in love with him. All of me. He's continued to break me open. He gets me to talk about the painful things *and* the beautiful things, right before he makes sweet, thorough love to me. He's as transformative and spiritually enlightening as he is physically mind-blowing.

I still haven't said the three little words I know he wants to hear, even though I show him every chance I get.

I can admit that there is one question I want answered. For a while, Chase was my entire world. I loved him the way only a fourteen-year-old girl who's just lost her father and feels scared and lonely can love: with a passion that borders on worship. For a long time I was convinced that he and I would be together again, that we would end up together and this is the way things were meant to be. It's a scenario that Chase has always—and especially lately—been feeding the flames of. He's convinced that Travis is my "world experience." He thinks I'm sowing my wild oats but that, deep down, I'm convinced Chase is my destiny.

I know better now.

But I want to see him again.

I already know how I'll feel but I'm curious.

Four years is a long time.

I sing my songs and it's strange to know he's out there in the crowd somewhere. I finish my set and then I join Travis on stage for his third song—our song, one we wrote together that's on my album. Then I head back to my dressing room. When the band has their intermission, Travis pulls me onto his lap and I give him a sip of whiskey straight from the bottle before kissing his lips. I love how he buzzes during his performances. Like he's made of pure, hot, male energy. "Get a room, you two," complains Vaughn, but then it's time for them to go back on for their second set.

It's only then, once Travis has gone, that I check my messages.

It's only then that I hear a knock on the door of my dressing room.

I go over and open it.

And I'm enveloped in a huge bear hug. He twirls me around and then sets me down and I can only stare at him. "Chase."

His palms rest on my bare shoulders and he gazes at me. All of me. "Ruby Hayes. Wow. Look at you. You are *so* beautiful."

"I can't believe it's you." He hasn't changed. He's still handsome, in a lanky, boyish kind of a way. Chase and I are almost exactly the same age. His birthday is one week before mine. He looks … young. I'm used to Travis's in-your-face masculinity, his seasoned virility and his alpha intensity that hits me right below my navel—among other places—every time I look at him.

Chase's effect is a lot more … calm.

"You were *amazing*, Ruby. Seriously," he beams at me, then his eyes rove lower. "And all grown up."

"How did you get in here?" The security surrounding the Tucker Brothers Band is usually airtight.

"You know I'm still in touch with Rose sometimes, right? She sent me her all-show backstage pass. She knew you wouldn't mind."

"Of course I don't mind. It's so good to see you, Chase."

"Come with me. I'm heading downtown with some friends I want you to meet. There's a band at this cool little hole-in-the-wall bar called Smoke. It's not far from here. They're waiting for us outside."

"I should probably wait for Travis."

"He'll be hours, though, right? Come on, we haven't seen each other in forever. I'm sure he won't mind."

I'm sure he *will* mind.

Chase gives me a teasing look. "Don't tell me he's got you on a short leash now. Wow. That's not the wild and free Ruby Hayes *I* know and love."

"He doesn't have me on a leash."

"Then come on. You can leave him a message and he can catch up with us later."

That doesn't sound unreasonable.

"What's the big deal?" Chase asks.

What *is* the big deal? I can go have a drink with my old friend who I haven't seen in four years.

Can't I?

Travis and I can spend an hour or two apart without the world coming to an end, right? He can trust me. There's nothing wrong with me going out with Chase and his friends while Travis's band finishes their second set. It's fine. "Okay. Sure. Let me put on some jeans."

Chase is still standing there beaming at me like he can't believe I've changed as much as I have. And I *have* changed. A lot. In every imaginable way.

"Do you mind, um, turning around for a second?"

Chase smiles at me. "Okay."

He turns and I shimmy out of my sequined gold dress and find a pair of jeans, a pink top and a pair of cowboy boots. "I'll just send a message to Travis." I know he doesn't have his phone on him when he's performing. But he'll see it when he's finished.

I'm going to a bar called Smoke with Chase and his friends. I'll see you a little later at the hotel. Please don't worry. I add a heart emoji and leave it at that. It's normal, I remind myself, to have friends when you're in a relationship, no matter how intense it is. I don't have to feel guilty. And I don't *want* to feel guilty.

"Let's go," I say.

A couple of the security guys look at me curiously as I'm leaving with Chase. One of them asks me if Travis knows I'm leaving. "Yes," I tell him. Or he will, soon enough.

We meet up with Chase's friends and he introduces me as we walk along the street toward the bar. His friends all stare at me like I've sprouted two heads. It occurs to me that I'm sort of famous now, maybe. I'm not used to their reactions. I haven't been in a normal setting since this whole whirlwind started and it feels different.

I miss Travis. I miss the security and brawn and warmth of his presence.

But I'm here now so I might as well try to enjoy myself.

We get to the bar and it's loud and packed with people and there's a band playing classic rock covers from a tiny corner stage. Chase gets me a drink and we sit in a booth with his friends and talk as much as we can over the noise. A few people stare at me but I do my best to blend in. It feels strange to be stared at.

"God, I missed you so much," Chase says again and I can't help thinking it: *if he missed me so much, why didn't he ever come back?* All those years I'd somehow thought it was *my* fault that we were apart. That it was my boarding school and my strict schedule that came between us. But it's occurring to me now that *Chase* wasn't at boarding school. He had a job throughout high school and all the freedom in the world. If he'd wanted to see me that badly, why hadn't he?

Travis would have come back, is what I'm thinking.

Travis never would have left in the first place.

An old Eagles song comes on and Chase reaches for my hand. "Remember this song, Roo? Remember that summer before I left when we spent so much time down by the river? We used to love this song."

We did love this song.

"Come dance with me," he says.

All his other friends are dancing and I figure why not so we go onto the dance floor and it's then that people really start noticing me. A girl takes a photo of me and I want to tell her not to do that.

Chase is holding me close—maybe *too* close—and I'm starting to feel sort of claustrophobic. It's so crowded in here.

There are a lot of people watching me. Curious women. Men with unnerving thoughts behind their eyes. Moving closer. I want to leave. I'm starting to realize that this isn't entirely safe. People recognize me and I've put myself in danger by coming here.

And that's when it happens.

Chase's palm eases around the nape of my neck and he kisses me, holding me there.

I freeze.

His lips are soft, moving gently against mine. And my curiosity is laid to rest. This kiss is meek and mild. It's my past. It feels empty and brotherly and wrong. It's not *him*. It doesn't have his passion and his fire. There's none of that raging, feral love behind it that ignites us both with a need we can't control.

I place my hand on Chase's chest and I pull back. "No, Chase," I tell him softly.

Somewhere outside of what's happening between me and Chase and all the realizations that are blazing along with it, I'm aware of a change in the atmosphere. Like a storm just blew in.

There's a lot of commotion.

The crowd has parted.

People are gasping and making sounds of awe and excitement.

He's flanked by his brothers and behind them is a brigade of beefy security guards.

He looks huge and suntanned and mad as a bull at a rodeo. And so gorgeous he takes my breath away.

Travis.

16

TRAVIS

WE TAKE our bows and leave the stage and I feel agitated for some reason.

I need to see her.

I check her dressing room but she's not there. She's not in mine either. I wander around, checking rooms, searching.

Calm down. You can handle not seeing her for an hour or two without self-detonating.

Where the fuck is she?

I go find my phone to check my messages.

I'm going to a bar called Smoke with Chase and his friends. I'll see you a little later at the hotel. Please don't worry x

A jolt of electric panic sears through my brain.

No.

"No what?" asks Kade. I didn't even realize I'd spoken it out loud.

I stay calm exactly long enough to google the name of the bar. It's only a block from the stadium. "Ruby went to a bar with that dipshit from her hometown who came to the show tonight." I'm breathing hard. I don't care about the guy. I'll fucking kill him. What I care about is that she's put herself in harm's way. She's new at this. She doesn't understand that people get rabid very quickly. Fans think they know a person from the photographs and the songs. They feel strangely possessive and overfamiliar and if people see her there, completely unprotected, they might—

I rush out and start running toward the door. I'm vaguely aware that Kade and Vaughn and maybe even Roxie are following me, yelling to people.

I'm sure it looks strange, us running the block or so to where the bar is located, trailed by ten hulking, out-of-breath bodyguards. I burst in through the door, not giving a shit about the bouncer, some vaping hipster I could easily take in a fight. I push past him.

"Hey," he says. But then he recognizes me. And my brothers.

So does everyone else in the bar. There are whispered gasps of recognition. The crowd parts for us.

And that's when I see her.

She's standing there on the crowded dance floor.

He's kissing her.

His hand is holding her there.

She gently pushes him away.

"No, Chase," she says. I can't hear the words but it's clear enough what's happening here.

It wouldn't surprise me if my blood, at that moment, literally boils.

Before I know what I'm even doing I'm on top of him, punching his face.

Somewhere at the edge of my rage, I hear her voice. *"Travis, stop! Please! Stop!"*

I get a few more punches in but vice-like hands grip me and pull me off. I fight them, *wanting to get my fucking hands on him again,* but there are too many of them.

"Travis," Vaughn is saying. "Calm the fuck down, man."

I'm being held back by several security guards and my brothers.

She's kneeling over him. He's a scrawny little punk. She helps him sit up and there's blood streaming down from his nose. He'll have a couple of decent shiners by morning.

Good.

He deserves more.

"Are you sure you're okay, Chase?" she's asking him.

"Ruby." She's the only thing I can see. "Are you all right, darlin'?" I need to know.

The kid's friends help him to his feet and someone gets him a wad of napkins for his nose. The bartender hands him some wrapped ice.

Ruby walks over to me. Her angel's face is flushed and

her golden eyes are furious. Even like this—or *especially* like this—she's stunning. I feel dizzy with relief and love and lust and this raging rush of protectiveness. My arms are still being held and she pokes her finger at my chest. "Why did you *do* that, Travis? You can't go around punching people like that!"

"He was kissing you."

Her angry little face is heart-breaking. I want to devour her scowling pink mouth like I've never wanted anything in my life. I want to come in her mouth. I want her to drink my seed as I flood her with it and wash every trace of him away. I want to imprint her with my life force. I want to marry her and wake up next to her every day for the rest of time.

"I could have handled it! I didn't need you rampaging in here like a lunatic!"

"*Handle* it? Was that you, *handling* it? *Letting* him do that? Did you *want* him to kiss you. Is that it?"

"No! I didn't *let* him! And I *didn't* want him to! You don't know anything."

I try to keep my cool but the fact is, the only thing holding me back from pummeling the little dipshit again is the steel-strong grip of several MMA-trained body-guards who are currently—barely—keeping me in check. "Ruby. There's no way in hell I was ever going to tolerate him touching you. Of course I wasn't. *Fuck*. You know me better than that by now."

"Yeah, Ruby," says someone from the crowd, almost

accusingly. We're surrounded by people, I notice. Many of them are filming us with their phones, like they're invested in what's going on here. "What did you expect him to do?"

She's still glaring at me.

"And if he so much as even *thinks* about laying a finger on you *ever* again—" I shoot him a menacing glance with a loaded threat packed into it. "I'll make him severely wish he hadn't in a slow and excruciatingly painful way." It comes out sounding more good-natured than homicidal. Because—and this is going to sound crazy, because it is—I'm happy. I still can't believe I've found the girl of my dreams. She's real and she's *beautiful*. Sassy as hell and gearing up for a fight, but I don't care. I'll listen, I'll agree, I'll do whatever it takes, as long as she's safe and she comes home with me. Those are two things I'll never compromise on.

Roxie's here and she puts her arm around Ruby and starts guiding her toward the door. "Let's go now, Ruby. Let's get you back to the hotel and you two can have it out there, okay? I think we've given the crowd enough viral footage for one night, don't you?"

We get outside and we're ushered into a limo that someone must have called and Ruby sits opposite me with her arms folded and a pissed off pout on her face.

I sit there watching her, drowning in my love for her, doing my best to survive it. I can't help it: I smile at her, half-remorsefully. "I'm not sorry," I tell her.

She bites her lip. The little furrow between her eyebrows is still there. "I can't believe you did that," she murmurs.

"Of course I did that, darlin'. And I'll do it again."

She's mad at me but something has changed in her. I can see it because it's the something I'm always looking for.

The shield. The thing she always held back. The part of herself she was protecting because she was scared or unsure.

It's gone.

17

My fists are still balled at my sides. I'm pacing. I think about calling Gi but it's late and I don't want to wake her.

As part of our tour allowances, Travis and I actually each get our own hotel rooms. I've never used mine before but tonight I asked Roxie if I could use my own. I need some time to think.

I'm still seething.

I'm still reeling.

Six weeks ago I'd never heard another person raise their voice, aside from petty arguments between my sisters. I'd never left the state of Tennessee or sung a song to another person or had sex or tasted whiskey or been in a bar crowded with people who were half-intrigued and half-predatory-in-a-way-that's-only-now-sinking-in. I'd never seen two people get in a fight. I'd never been kissed on a dance floor or fought over. I'd never confronted my past and my present so jarringly. I'd never been in love.

I'd never had the realization that I've met the person I want to spend the rest of my life with, even though I'm young and there's a big wide world out there and all kinds of experiences to be had.

I don't want any of it without him.

He's become the sun.

And I never meant for that to happen.

But it has.

So much so that he's burning me even now. We're *each other's* suns, white-hot and revolving around each other, merging and sparking off each other's heat while everything else feels small and distant and cold in comparison.

It's a lot and I need a minute.

I look out to the murky industrial skyline and the sea beyond it. The layer on layer grayness of the view makes me feel lonely. This place is so foreign to me tonight. I miss my home.

I miss Travis madly.

I'm still not sure I've entirely forgiven him.

For what?

For risking his own safety to make sure I was okay?

I don't want to be controlled.

Then again, he wasn't really trying to control me. He was fighting for me, even if I didn't need him to.

Chase shouldn't have kissed me.

But I'm glad he did.

Now I know.

Now I don't have to wonder.

And I imagine how *I* would feel, if I'd walked in on Travis getting kissed by some past love on a dance floor.

I would fight for him too. Of course I would.

So why did I expect him to sit back and watch me figure out if I still had feelings for Chase or not? It wasn't fair.

My phone buzzes in my pocket. I pull it out and see Roxie's name on the screen. "Hi, Roxie."

"I just want to check on you and make sure you're okay."

"I am. Thanks."

"Are you still mad at him?"

I stare out at the view. "No."

"Good." A long pause. "Ruby? He was always going to react to that. He's not going to share you. He never was. He loves you and he's obsessed with you and he'll do anything for you."

Tears pool in my eyes.

I know.

"And when I say he loves you, I mean he *loves* you. He's insane with it. We have never, ever seen him fall like this. Not once. Not even close."

I feel the slide of a tear down my cheek. It's a tear of realization. Of magnitude. Of understanding that your soulmate walks the earth and loves you at least as hard as you love him, which only compounds the whole thing exponentially. "Where is he?"

"He's right outside your door."

"What?"

"He was sitting there for a while but I think he fell asleep. He was never going to leave you. And he didn't want you to leave without him knowing about it." Her voice is gentle but layered with emotion. I get the feeling she's worried about her brother. "You two can work this out, Ruby. I know you can. Be careful with him. You're holding his heart in your hands."

He was never going to leave you.

I'm not sure what I did to deserve Travis Tucker's love but I decide right here and now to finally and totally *let it in*. To stop trying to define it or treat it like something that's holding me back. Travis has *never* held me back. He's given me wings and roots and more pleasure and opportunity and wild love than I know what to do with.

"I promise I will, Roxie. I'll be careful with him. I love him."

"I know you do. I can see it. That performance tonight was your best ever, by the way. Tomorrow's your day off and I don't want to see either one of you until you've worked this out. Okay?"

"Okay."

We end the call. I take a deep breath. I walk over to the door and I open it.

The movement of the door wakes him but he almost topples into the room.

His eyes are bloodshot, making the green of his irises

look off-neon with rims of jade. His hair's a glorious mess. His half-smile is the most beautiful thing I've ever seen.

"Hi," I say.

"Hi."

"Do you … want to come in?"

"Okay." He gets to his feet, kicking the door closed. We stand there facing each other for a few seconds. His shirt is dirty from the bar room brawl. Against the dark denim of his rolled up cuff there's a smear of Chase's blood. He wears a thick black leather bracelet with a sort of pocket where he keeps spare guitar picks. His forearms are muscular and tanned. There's a bruise across his knuckle.

"I love you," I say.

He stares down at me with so much heartfelt emotion, his eyes are bright with it in the low light.

He picks me up and carries me to the bed where he undresses me slowly as he peels off his own clothes, kissing me, whispering words as his mouth devours me worshipfully. *I love you so much, Ruby.* His mouth closes over my nipple and he draws hungrily, tugging softly with his teeth, running his tongue around the taut, sensitive nub. Each flick sends a molten current of heat to my warm pussy. Gripping me with his strong hands, he licks and kisses a line down my stomach. *I'm going to make you so happy. I'm going to love you so hard you won't know what hit you.* He parts the soft lips of my pussy, very gently skating his fingers over my clit. *You're so beautiful, my sweet baby.* As he does this, I grip his thick cock with its roping veins, sliding my fingertips over the pearl of pre-cum at the tip. It surges, spilling another gush as I slide my fist along his length. *I want to live inside you for the rest of time, darlin'.* I pull him closer, so crazy in lust and love that I *need* him now. He slides his big cock deep inside my body and I wrap my arms and legs around him and pull him as close as I can. *Oh, fuck, I love you.* I weave my fingers through his hair and kiss his perfect mouth.

We say the words over and over as the pleasure bonds us, body and soul, in a squeezing, gushing rush from which we never quite recover.

EPILOGUE

Ruby

MAYBE OUR FATES were already sealed, that day by the pond when we connected that very first time. I still think there was something magical about our feverish, sticky bond in the heat of that summer day, when I first tasted him, when he first imprinted me with his lust and his love. Every glance, every kiss and every note only fed our addiction until now we can't bear to be apart.

Travis has been true to his word. Not only does he never leave me, but we've been inseparable, well, since the day we met.

Most of the time we live in Nashville at the loft and at another house he has that sort of blew my mind the first time I saw it. It's in Franklin and is basically a castle. It had become overrun with friends and a party scene that was one of the things that fed his and his band's fame in the first place, like a non-stop music video. It wasn't a place he spent much time, but now Travis is talking about doing some work to it so we can raise our babies there. I told him he'll have to wait a few years for that, but secretly I don't think it'll be too long. The women in my family tend to have babies young and I probably will too. But not yet.

Travis got down on his knee on the last night of our tour and proposed to me in front of a sold out crowd.

I said yes.

Then he slid the biggest ruby ring I've ever seen on my finger and I haven't taken it off since.

We promised my Momma we'd get married by the pond and make a good party out of it. We decided to set the date for my twentieth birthday. Until then we're going to travel and tour and make beautiful music together.

Travis had the barn at his country house sound-proofed and we've been writing and recording there, hanging out with his family, who all spend a lot of time there. They've become like my own family and we all have Sunday lunch together when they're there. My Momma can't get enough of them and she cooks up a feast for them every chance she gets.

The Tucker Brothers Band's fourth album went platinum. So did their fifth.

And so did my second.

Travis got a tattoo of my name inked across his chest,

over his heart. And another one of the first three notes I sang to him across his wrist, where his pulse can be felt. I got a tiny TT on my shoulder.

Travis and Chase called a truce, once I had the ring on my finger. Travis is still surly at times about it but I'm pretty good at placating him. I just tell him I love him *as* I make love to him and he always comes around.

He's my rock and my anchor, my dream lover and my best friend. I write songs about him and kiss him all day long. I'm so in love with him it scares me, to be *this* emotionally, spiritually and physically attached to my beautiful hunky rock star fiancé. But he just tells me he loves me *as* he makes love to me and it calms me and makes me believe that true love really can last a lifetime.

Chase and I message each other from time to time. Our friendship will always have a special place in my heart but it's something that feels more a part of the past than it ever did about the present, or the future.

Rose met an app developer named Tyler who's a lot nerdier than the men she used to go for, but he thinks she walks on water and he also has more money than God. He proposed a month after they met and she was pregnant a month after that. I've never seen her happier.

Scarlett called a week later to say that they'd just found out she was pregnant with twins.

Momma met a farmer from the other side of town at a dinner club she started going to and has been on a few dates with him. His name is Earl and he plays an old fiddle. He's actually had a couple of jam sessions with the brothers after our Sunday lunches and he's damn good. They've even talked about getting him to accompany one of the songs on their next album.

Travis's three cousins, Gage, Caleb and Bo all came for Christmas with their wives, Luna, Violet and Millie, and we had the best four days together. We spent the whole time eating and drinking, taking walks, playing pool and laughing. They're amazing people with big hearts, interesting lives and a real care for each other that's both endearing and fun to be a part of. One thing I'm learning about Travis and his family: they love hard and once they've fallen, they're all in.

Kade got his own love story, which was as entertaining to watch as it was dramatic. Stella has become one of my best friends. But that's a story for another day …

Roxie also got her love story, and one that might be the closest thing to a fairy tale I've ever heard of …

As for Gigi, she's working on a degree in social work. Her first day of practical work happened to coincide with the day Travis, Roxie and Kade booked Vaughn into rehab for an intervention he insisted he didn't need. He says his excesses are a case of an overload of energy he needs an outlet for.

We'll see.

But if there's anyone on this earth who can fix him, it's Gigi, although the two of them are about as compatible as oil and water. Or at least that's what I used to think. I remember that first time they met in our kitchen, thinking that Gigi and Vaughn would be the worst match in history. As it turns out, once Vaughn fell—and fell *hard* —he'd do absolutely anything and everything to change her mind about him. We're all waiting to find out if he can. My guess is yes …

Thank you so much for reading **Nashville Days**. If you enjoyed Travis and Ruby's story, please consider leaving a quick review or rating on Amazon.

Below I've included the first chapter of **Nashville Nights**, the next book in the Music Lovers series— Vaughn's book! I fell in love with Vaughn as I was writing his story. Gigi is the calm to his storm and I loved the empathy in her character and the balance she brought to her wild alpha rockstar.

xoxo,
Julie

Please come join my Facebook reader group, Julie Capulet's Romantics, where I share cover reveals, insider info and we discuss all things romance!

Sign up for my newsletter to receive my free bonus content and get access to sneak peeks and exclusive giveaways!

Visit my website @ www.juliecapulet.com

He's *crazy* for her …

Vaughn Tucker is the hot as hell drummer of the Tucker Brothers band, whose four albums have all hit number one. Vaughn is drop-dead gorgeous … and completely out of control.

Gigi Hayes's life is a million miles from packed stadiums and high-profile tour schedules. She's a small-town girl who spends all her time working in the library and studying to become a qualified social worker. For … reasons.

When Vaughn meets Gigi, for the first time in his life, he's the one who's star-struck. But Gigi is saving herself for true love. And even though she's drawn to the trouble-written-all-over-him superstar, she's not deluded enough to believe he's capable of such a thing.

Vaughn has already fallen hard. And Gigi's refusals only make him crazier. She's an angel and he may as well be the devil himself.

But when heaven meets hell, all bets are off …

Nashville Nights is a sexy standalone rockstar romance starring an out-of-control drummer and the one woman who's everything he never knew he needed.

Music City Lovers

Chapter One

VAUGHN

I wake up to the sound of birds chirping.

Where the …?

My head is pounding hellishly.

A vivid image of my mother's face fringes at the edge of my awareness. Her dark hair and her green eyes. *I love you, Vaughn.* It's the very last thing she ever said to me.

My eyes are suddenly wide open.

Her image fades but it's jarring. The heaviness of the loss of her is as raw as it ever was. It never seems to soften or fade out.

I look around.

I'm in a barn, sleeping in a goddamn pile of hay.

Which is surprisingly comfortable.

I crashed out after an all-nighter with my brothers, I remember now. We wrote three complete songs.

And drank a lot of whiskey.

Too much whiskey, if my hangover is any judge.

The place is huge, with dusty beams and an old-timey, rustic vibe. Morning sunlight streams through thin gaps in the wood, painting the whole place in stripes of … beauty, maybe. The kind that makes you feel deeply, fully inspired, I realize as I lie here. Absorbing it.

You're a beautiful soul, Vaughn. Don't be reckless. Don't throw it all away.

Shit.

Having my mother speak to me knowingly from beyond the grave is not something I had on my bingo card this morning.

But I'm feeling it. Too deeply, as always. It's a pain I do my best to numb whenever the need arises. I slide my flask out of my back pocket and check its contents. Hair of the dog and all that. But it's empty.

I look almost eerily like my father did but people used to say my mother and I had the same personality. She was fun and enchanting to be around but there was a pronounced vulnerability to her character that was all about her kindness. She cared too much.

I don't see those similarities in myself at all. Unfortunately, my habits mirror all my father's worst tendencies. No matter how much I wish I wasn't, I basically *am* my father. And it's this realization that makes me want to self-medicate like nothing else does.

Whatever. I don't feel like analyzing my personality flaws this early in the morning. Or ever, more accurately.

I'm covered in straw and I'm dusty as fuck but the slant of the sunlight feels different today. Soft and colorful. Almost magical.

I must be really hungover.

I climb out of the hay and try to brush some of it off my clothes but to hell with it.

When I step outside into the daylight, the world is basically on fire with blazing sun, blue sky and green, rolling landscape as far as the eye can see. I have to shield my eyes for a few seconds from the glaring brightness of it all.

There's a pond in the distance.

Now there's an offer I can't refuse.

I take a few seconds to adjust to the sunlight and to make sure my equilibrium is more or less intact, then I walk down toward the pond, half-amazed at how scenic this place is. I've spent too much time in the city lately, on tour buses and in hotel rooms. It's good to get away from all that.

I'm running commando so I strip down and wade into the water, which is clear and clean-looking, and dive under.

Damn, it feels good.

I swim for a while and wash off the dirt and the sweat.

It's been a crazy few months on tour. I've overindulged in every way it's possible to overindulge. I've played my heart out and squeezed every last drop out of each day and—even more—each night.

It's just how I happen to live my life. Fast. Hard. Might as well make the most of the more-money-than-I-could-spend-in-this-lifetime, the whiskey on tap, the God-given gifts I happen to appreciate the hell out of. I have blue eyes and black hair. I'm 6'3" and built as fuck—in every regard. Women give me whatever I want whenever I want it. I thank my lucky stars for all of the above by enjoying the ride every chance I get. Why wouldn't I?

I'm famous, not just because I was recently listed among the top five drummers in the world but also because I tend to make headlines for a variety of reasons.

I prefer to let my fire burn bright.

I'm borderline out of control, maybe, but who isn't?

Anyone who tells me they're *in* control is full of shit, I figure. Even if such a thing was possible, it wouldn't be something I would aspire to. I have zero interest in living my life by a set of arbitrary rules that might be considered "acceptable."

To who?

No one *I* happen to know or care much about the opinion of, is what I've come to realize.

Even so, I can admit I feel sort of wrecked. Not just

physically, from all the insane excesses. Those are easy enough to bounce back from. I'm 24 and brimming with virile energy and blazing lust. It burns hot and borderline feral, all the time, so if I don't *use* it I feel like I might spontaneously fucking combust.

It's the existential exhaustion that hits harder. Sometimes it dawns on me that it would actually be nice to care about what other people think of me.

But all those impulses died on one particular stormy night, years ago now. Its effect still has the ability to exhaust me from time to time. Lately the memories have felt like more of a black cloud than usual. Having my mother revisit me in a surprisingly realistic hallucination out of the blue makes me realize how jaded I am. Maybe I'm closer to the edge than I thought.

The cool water feels nothing less than miraculous, like I'm somehow in the process of being reborn.

After a while, I walk up the sandy beach and grab my clothes but I don't bother putting them on. I'll dry off in the sun. There's no one around. I happen to be a person who's intensely comfortable in my own skin, with good reason. I don't know if I'm arrogant or just secure enough to know from experience that I happen to look like a guy who can show a girl the time of her life on around ten different levels. And then deliver on each and every one of those promises in spades. At least for one night.

That's just the way it is.

I notice, up a slope, there's a cottage situated in a

small grove of trees. Travis mentioned that there were two or three of them, along with the main house and the barn. Part of the property he bought only days ago. He wants me to move into one of the cabins for a while.

I know my family worries about me. I take things further than either of my brothers or my sister. Travis and Kade mostly stick to whiskey and Roxie doesn't drink at all.

But, hell, we all have our demons and we all handle them with different medicinal remedies. I tell them there's nothing to worry about.

I walk up the slope to check out the cabin.

It's got a small front porch with two wooden chairs and a nice view over the pond and the hills. I'm mostly dry so I pull on my jeans but leave them half-zipped. I toss my shirt onto one of the chairs and check the door. It's unlocked.

Whoever Travis bought the property from left everything behind, like they were planning to come back to it but never did. The house is furnished and so is this cabin. It's rustic and dusty but fully equipped as a guest house with all the modern conveniences. There's a small kitchen, a table next to the window, leather couches and a fireplace. There's one bedroom with a king-sized bed and a small but luxe bathroom.

Perfect.

There are even paintings on the walls. One is a geometric design, in black and white. It doesn't really go with the rustic furnishings or the wood of the interior, but I like it. It shakes things up.

After our next tour, which is only twelve shows, I might settle down right here and Jack Kerouac my way through a couple of weeks to see if I can create some music that digs so deep it goes down in infamy for the rest of time.

Or something.

All three of us write music and we all have different styles. Travis's is more country, Kade's leans toward bluegrass-meets-edgy-folk and mine is more rock 'n roll.

Yeah, that's what I'll do. Write. Let the angst and the regret and the feverish love of life pour out of me without distractions.

I find it interesting that the urge to write feels remarkably like lust. It's a spiritual lust but it spills over into a physical lust that's fiery and more voracious than any other kind.

Right now, I'm feeling it. I want to write something down and then fuck my way leisurely through a steamy afternoon with some willing nymph. Of which there are always plenty. Except that I'm out in the middle of the countryside and around fifty miles from civilization.

So I'll start with the writing, which can only be good if I'm feeling as feverish as I do right now.

Here I am, standing in the doorway of my new digs, leaning my shoulder against the doorjamb, jeans only partly zipped, appreciating the view as I contemplate the

state of my own raging lust, when into that view walks …
down by the pond … a girl.

Shit.

For a second I wonder if she's paparazzi. The last
thing I need is for fans to start camping out in the woods.
Or photos of me half naked all over the internet.

It wouldn't be the first time. Roxie sued some girl over
a leaked photo that was taken of me about a year ago. It
was eventually removed, but women still mention it to me
from time to time. I don't remember it being taken but
apparently it was memorable.

But I can't see a phone in her hand. Or a camera.

She's carrying a book.

And she hasn't seen me yet.

But then, as she walks along the track toward me, she
feels my gaze. She looks up at me. And she stops walking.

She's a distance away and I can't clearly see all the
finer details of her face. It's enough, though. She's cute.
In fact … hell. She's dressed in a faded pair of jeans and
a white button-down shirt, tied at the waist. Her hair,
which is pulled up off-handedly, is a light, vibrant shade
of red. It's what you'd call strawberry blond. The term
could have been invented just for her. She's wearing a pair
of black-framed glasses. I find myself wishing she wasn't.
They're hiding her face. But even from this distance I can
see a warm blush coloring her cheeks as she stares up
at me.

I imagine what I might look like to her. I glance down

out of curiosity. I'm mostly decent. At least I'm partly dressed, even if I am half-cocked. Which can't be helped. That's just how I live my life and there's not a damn thing I can do about it.

She's shocked by my presence. She wasn't expecting anyone to be here.

Who is she?

Where's she going?

I want to know.

"Hey," I yell out, raising my hand in a sort of greeting.

She doesn't wave back. Or answer me. She walks backwards for a few steps before turning in the direction she came from.

I almost laugh. "Wait."

She doesn't.

I zip myself mostly up and I start walking down the hill.

I don't want to scare her but, fuck, she can't just wander into my view like that in all her strawberry glory and expect me not to at least want to find out who she is. I'm too amped up to stand there while she walks away.

She follows a trail on the far side of the pond. She glances back to make sure I'm not following her. When she discovers I *am* following her—and in fact gaining on her in ground-eating strides she'll have to take off in a full run to possibly escape—she stops and turns to face me, her thick book hugged in front of her chest like a shield.

As I walk closer I can see that, behind her glasses, her large golden eyes are wide.

I exhale a laugh. "Shit. Don't be scared of me."

Then again, when you look how this girl looks, all pure and sun-touched and gently studious, maybe she *should* be scared. I'm tatted up to the nines, built as fuck and wild with lust and life. I probably weigh twice what she weighs. I'm suntanned and barefoot and shirtless.

She checks me out slowly, lingering on the tats on my arms and my chest. My stomach. The way the top button of my jeans still isn't fastened. To my face. My hair.

I can't tell if she recognizes me. She's not fangirling or swooning. There's a thread of curiosity, like something about me seems vaguely familiar but she can't quite place it. I don't want to break that bubble. I don't want her to freeze or to run.

"I'm sorry," she says, and I realize I got the wrong impression. She's not scared. She's feisty. Ready to fight.

Which makes me smile. The last thing I want to do is *fight* with this gorgeous little stranger who, now that I get a better look, is not just cute but seriously stunning in an I-wake-up-in-the-morning-looking-like-this kind of way. She's as natural as the sun-bright hayseeds waving in the wind and her hair is the exact same color. She has long, gold-tipped eyelashes that blink at me from behind her glasses, mesmerizingly smooth skin and the kind of plump, bee-stung lips that crank my half-cocked problem several notches higher. I feel hot and hungry to eat her mouth and can only hope like hell I don't bust out of my barely-fastened jeans.

I could sling her over my shoulder and carry her home with me. She couldn't stop me.

"I'm trespassing." Her voice is soft. Calming. It's the kind of voice that could soothe your nightmares or talk you off a ledge. "I didn't know anyone was here."

"You can trespass any time you want."

Her gaze wanders again over the many tattoos across my chest and lands on the smallest, a single word inked over my heart. I'm surprised when she asks it. "Who's Savannah?"

I don't answer right away. I wasn't expecting it, the weight of the name spoken in this girl's gentle voice, handled so carefully.

"My mother," I finally say, and my voice sounds more husky than usual.

She watches my eyes for a few seconds and through her glasses I can see that her tiger-yellow irises have a kindness and depth to them that makes me want to … do something. To dive in. To lose myself in the comfort of her.

"I have to go," she says. "It was nice … running into you. Bye now."

Bye now. "Wait. What's your name?"

She half-smiles and starts walking away, not even giving me that.

I walk along with her. I hold one of my wrists behind

my back as I walk. Hiding my fist, which is clenched for no particular reason. So I don't seem as threatening to her as I feel.

Her clothes aren't particularly tight-fitting but do little to hide the fact that she's got the kind of body that could —and just might—make a grown man cry. Curvy and lush. Her shirt is tied at the front, revealing a thin strip around her waist that shows off the smooth skin of her stomach. Her jeans are fitted around her hips but slightly looser around her waist, leaving a small gap at the front between her waistband and her skin. That little space, for some crazy reason, is … insanely tantalizing.

I want to touch her there, and slide my fingers inside, gliding over her soft pussy, getting her wet, playing her clit, slipping inside.

Fucking hell.

"I'll be away for a few weeks but then I'm moving into the cabin," I tell her. "Give me your number."

I never ask girls for their numbers. Or follow them. *Or* call after them. I don't need to.

We get to a fence. She climbs over it, ignoring my question. "This is me. I hope you have a nice trip."

She's dismissing me?

She's dismissing me. As she should. She's clearly wholesome and good. Clean and pure with golden aspirations and kind-hearted intentions.

The unfamiliarity of this situation amuses me for a couple of seconds. Every woman I've ever met has gone to lengths even I'm sometimes shocked by, to get my attention, to get into my bed, to taste, feel and own every inch of me they can get their hands on.

As for this one, for her, I'm a big black hole of experiences she doesn't yet know she needs.

"Tell me your name or I'm climbing over this fence and banging on your door until you tell me." She gives me a look that's slightly exasperated or maybe even annoyed and this, for some reason, makes my chest sort of ache, with … I don't know. It feels almost like happiness.

"What's yours?" she asks me.

Her mouth, holy hell. It's making me feel depraved. *I want to kiss her. Taste her lips. More than that. I want to spill myself all over her and inside her. I want to lick her and eat her and fuck her until she's crying because I'm so deep and I feel so damn good.*

"Vaughn." I almost say my last name, but hold it, in case she still isn't sure.

It's enough. A little crinkle appears between her eyebrows and those flags of pink warm her face again. Like it just clicked. She recognizes me. "I have to go."

I don't want her to leave me yet. I climb the fence and, because there's a huge tree next to it, I sling myself up onto a thick, low branch.

"You'll fall," she says. "You don't even have shoes on." The sound of her bell-toned Tennessee twang is just about the sweetest thing I've heard in a long time. I'm not sure why. Her feisty, gently-scolding delivery is getting me hot. Even hotter than I already was. My cock is now fully hard and borderline painful and my jeans still aren't fully done up.

I want to lay her down in the summer grass and kiss those pillowy lips. Peel off her clothes. Run my tongue around her nipples until they're taut and ripe for me. Until she's moaning. I want to find out if she's strawberry blond everywhere. And rub my hard, bursting cock against her pink pussy until she's all slippery and ready for me …

Fuck.

Calm down, you maniac.

This hotness feels tangled. With a weirdly wild joy and a craving. For her to fix those golden eyes onto me with all their kind depth and sassy gorgeousness.

For her to care.

I want her to scold me again.

I want to do things that shock her and make her *feel* me. My lust and my pain.

I'm sitting on this tree branch six or so feet off the ground and from here I can see the back door of her house. It's red. "I just want to know what your name is. Since we're neighbors now."

Her eyes are studying me softly and I'd pay a million dollars to hear what she's thinking right now. "Gigi," she finally says.

Gigi. I love that. "It's nice to meet you, Gigi."

"Nice to meet you too, Vaughn. Now will you please get down?"

"You can walk through that land anytime you want. Swim. Walk the trails. Spend time in my cabin, if you need some time alone to read your book. Anything you want. We'll be gone for a few weeks."

She barely tilts her head, like she's surprised by my offer. "Thanks."

I jump down, landing on the soft grass. She watches me do this, taking in the dirt on my jeans from the bark and my bare, inked, suntanned chest. She's staring at me like she's wary I might be borderline crazy.

She's right.

My phone rings in my back pocket.

She takes this as her cue. "Bye, Vaughn," she says.

"Maybe I'll see you when I get back."

I take my phone out of my pocket, but I'm watching her as she walks away. As I do this, a wave of loneliness hits me right in the middle of my chest that clashes with the bright light of the sunny day. Maybe my flashback is having its way with me again.

Fuck.

I need a drink.

I look at the phone still ringing in my hand. It's Travis. "Hey."

"You up? We're leaving soon."

"Yeah. I'll be there in twenty." I hang up on him. He's distracting me.

I'm still watching Gigi as she walks up the steps of her

house, glancing back to see me standing right where she left me.

My new tiger-eyed neighbor.

Chances are I'll forget about her by the time I get back from our tour.

Maybe.

Not a chance in hell.

What I find myself thinking is … I want to make her blush again. And show her how good my kind of trouble feels.

I want to hear the feisty little stranger with the sun-bright hair and the flags of warmth on her face moan my name as she comes hard around me.

Watch out, strawberry girl.

What I want, I always get.

"All I wished for was to experience that spark you read about, just once. What I wasn't expecting was the Fourth of July and heaven on earth all rolled into one." ~ Stella

Bass player Kade Tucker is known as the Magic Man, and not only for his riffs. After breaking off a disastrous relationship, he swears off women. Only problem is, five minutes later, he might have just met the love of his life.

Stella Bell has always done what's expected of her. Until a secret letter and an unwanted proposal on the same day prove to be her breaking point. For once in her life, she's going to do something for herself. As fate would have it, that means taking a spur of the moment trip to Nashville.

A hopeless romantic, Stella has been hiding her true self for far too long. And when a gorgeous, mysterious stranger rescues her from a torrential downpour, she decides to go with it. The hot, dreamy Kade Tucker enlightens Stella in every possible way, until she begins to realize that some dreams really can come true.

But will Kade's twisted ex and Stella's family secrets – and a very accidental pregnancy – get in the way of their HEA?

Or is this a match made in Music City heaven?

Nashville Dreams is a sexy standalone rockstar romance starring a hot musician and a sweet & sassy dreamer who's the one he always knew was out there somewhere. Now that he's found her, he has no intention of letting any one of her dreams go unanswered.

Music City Lovers

Roxie

Nate Boone. My brother's best friend and the country boy I had a serious crush on all those years ago when we were both just kids. A lot has happened since then but a part of me never really moved on. Who am I kidding, *all* of me never moved on.

And now I'm heading back to Sugar Mountain to see my bestie—Nate's little sister—and to catch up with the extended Boone family, who have always felt like my own.

What I find is that Nate Boone is *alll* grown up, hotter than the Tennessee sun and not quite as forbidden as he used to be …

Nate

Roxie Tucker. No one knows about our history and our connection because I walked away and never looked back. I had to. She was a hundred percent off-limits.

I haven't seen her in years, until she shows up out of the blue, so beautiful it hurts. And I now know why I could never get real or even think about committing to anyone else. Because they're not her.

I shouldn't, of course. She's like family. And my life is complicated.

But she's too perfect and the pull is too strong. She's my dream and the one I could never let go of. I lost her once and I have no intention of losing her again. She's mine. She's heaven on earth and I'm a hundred percent addicted.

Now that I've had a taste of forever, this time, I'll risk whatever it takes to keep her...

Nashville Lights is a steamy standalone small town brother's best friend romance, starring a sweet & sassy band manager and the love of her life.

Music City Lovers

ALSO BY JULIE CAPULET

I Love You Series

The Obsession Begins (free)

XOXO I Love You

XOXX I Love You More

Love You the Most (free)

Sexy Standalones

Max

Cowboy

McCabe Brothers Series

Hopeless Romantic

My Hero

Arrogant Player

Music City Lovers Series

Nashville Days

Nashville Nights

Nashville Dreams

Nashville Lights

Hawthorne U Series

Lovestruck

Paradise Series

Devil's Angel

Wild Hearts

New York Billionaires Series

Billionaire Boss

Billionaire Grump

Billionaire Devil

Billionaire Romantic

Standalone Romcom

Beautiful Savages

ABOUT THE AUTHOR

Julie Capulet is an Amazon top 20 bestselling author of contemporary romance. She writes steamy he-falls-first romance with heart, heat and fairy tale HEAs. Her stories are inspired by true love and she's married to her own real life hero. When she's not writing, she's reading, traveling, walking on the beach and watching rom-coms.

www.juliecapulet.com

www.ingramcontent.com/pod-product-compliance
Lightning Source LLC
Chambersburg PA
CBHW061225310726
48971CB00007B/1941